Whispers of the Enchanting Dark

The Dark Secrets of Fairy Tales

Book Cover by Angeless Watkins-Gallar

Illustrations by Angeless Watkins-Gallar

ISBN
979-8-3303-6938-6 (Paperback)
979-8-3303-6942-3 (eBook)

ANGELESS WATKINS-GALLAR

Angeless began his journey in a small town in Wiltshire after his parents needed to move for his father's work. It was there that he spent his formative years, navigating the challenges of dyslexia, which, rather than serving as a hindrance, fuelled his vivid imagination, allowing him to find solace in looking beyond the written words, enabled him to delve into the intricacies of characters, feeling their emotions, and immersing in their stories.

Despite the hurdles posed by dyslexia in expressing himself through writing, Angeless discovered alternative outlets such as art to convey his thoughts and emotions. This creative exploration laid the foundation for a unique perspective that would later shape his approach to storytelling.

After two decades in the fast-paced realm of Information Technology, it was a pivotal moment in 2019 that prompted a significant shift in his mindset. Seeking a deeper connection with others and inspired by a desire to contribute positively to mental health, he embarked on a journey of self-discovery and education.

Studying Mental Health and Wellbeing courses became a transformative experience, leading him to attain qualifications in Mental Health and counselling. The realisation that his life skills and newfound knowledge could help to help others prompted the decision to further his training as a humanistic life coach. Armed with a combination of personal experiences and professional training, Angeless soon made a meaningful impact on the lives of those seeking guidance. However, this marked the start of a new chapter in his life.

Angeless delved into the world of fairy tales, found himself compelled to explore the hidden depths beyond the surface narrative.
The result is his debut work, " (Whispers of the Enchanted Dark: The Dark Secrets of Fairy Tales)," a venture into the mystical and often overlooked aspects of these timeless stories.

And now, fully embracing his dyslexia rather than it serving him as a hinderance, it has allowed him to write and continue to write and to form characters with a deep and meaningful passion.

In the enchanting world of fairy tales, where magic and wonder abound, lies a dark undercurrent that often goes unnoticed. Beyond the whimsical façade of talking animals, beautiful princesses, and happily-ever-afters, there exists a realm of horrors and hidden meanings that most parents dare not reveal to their innocent children.

For centuries, these timeless tales have captivated the imaginations of young and old alike, transporting us to far-off lands where anything is possible. Yet, concealed within their narratives are cautionary tales, steeped in symbolism and laden with darker truths. These are the stories that resonate deeply within our souls, stirring emotions we may not fully comprehend.

But why, you may ask, would parents choose to shield their children from the true horrors that lie with-in these tales?

The answer is both simple and complex. It is a delicate balance between preserving innocence and sheltering them from the harsh realities of the world. Fairy tales, in their original forms, were never meant for tender ears or fragile minds.

They were born from a time when life was unforgiving, and the world itself was a treacherous place.

Behind the cheerful façade of a dancing princess or a mischievous talking cat, lies a cautionary message, a stark reminder of the dangers that lurk in the shadows.

These tales explore themes of betrayal, loss, abandonment, and the consequences of making ill-informed choices.

They serve as metaphors for the trials and tribulations we encounter in our own lives, often echoing the fears and struggles we face as we navigate the treacherous path to adulthood.

These hidden meanings, woven into the fabric of the tales, speak to our deepest fears and desires. They serve as mirrors, reflecting the complexities of the human experience and offering us a glimpse into the depths of our own psyche.

By exploring the horrors within these stories, we come face to face with the darkness that resides within us all. However, it is precisely because of these horrors that fairy tales hold a unique power.

They allow us to confront our fears in a safe and controlled environment, providing us with a sense of catharsis and a roadmap for resilience. Through the trials and tribulations of the characters, we find hope, courage, and the strength to overcome our own demons.

In this book, we not only dare to reveal the horrors and hidden meanings behind beloved fairy tales, but we also delve into the intricate web of emotions and psychological complexities that shape these stories.

Beyond the surface-level narratives, we explore the depths of human experiences, uncovering the traumas, fears, and desires that often remain unspoken.

Each fairy tale serves as a portal to a different realm of psychological exploration.

We peer into the twisted psyche of Little Red Riding Hood, who grapples with her own duality of innocence and temptation.

We unravel the psychological torment endured by Cinderella, who battles feelings of worthlessness and yearns for validation. We delve into the dark recesses of Snow White's mind as she confronts her own mortality and fears of aging.

Through these journeys, we encounter the raw and unfiltered aspects of the human psyche, exposing the fragility and resilience that coexist within us all.

As we navigate these tales, we come face to face with the ghosts of trauma, the haunting memories that shape our lives. We examine the psychological impact of abandonment in Hansel and Gretel, as they venture into the depths of the forest, desperate to find their way home.

We witness the transformation of Beauty in Beauty and the Beast, as she learns to see beyond external appearances and confront her own insecurities.

Each tale serves as a mirror, reflecting our own fears, desires, and struggles, and inviting us to confront them head-on.

Moreover, we delve into the complex dynamics of power, control, and manipulation that underlie many fairy tales.

The wicked stepmothers, evil queens, and malevolent witches serve as embodiments of psychological manipulation, often preying upon the vulnerabilities of the protagonists.

We explore the ways in which these figures manipulate, gaslight, and coerce their victims, leaving deep psychological scars that resonate long after the stories conclude.

In our exploration of the horrors and hidden meanings, we also shine a light on the resilience and empowerment that can emerge from within.

We witness the transformation of the protagonists as they navigate their own psychological labyrinths, finding strength, courage, and self-discovery along the way. Through their journeys, we are reminded that even in the face of darkness, there is always the potential for growth and transformation.

As we embark on this psychological journey, we invite you to question, reflect, and explore the nuances of these timeless tales.

We encourage you to delve deeper into the emotions, the traumas, and the hidden depths that lie within the fairy tales we thought we knew so well.

Prepare to confront the shadows within, for it is in facing our own fears and vulnerabilities that we can truly understand the power of these stories.

So, step into the pages of this book and let us embark on a psychological exploration of the fairy tales that have both enchanted and haunted us.

Together, we will unravel the mysteries, confront the horrors, and uncover the profound truths that lie within.

Brace yourself for a journey into the depths of the human psyche, where the fairy tales we thought we knew will be forever transformed.

I would like to express my deepest gratitude to the brilliant minds behind the fairy tales that have captivated generations: the Brothers Grimm, Hans Christian Andersen, Charles Perrault, John Ruskin, and the creators of the Arabian Nights. Your timeless tales have served as the foundation and inspiration for this reimagining of the fairy tale genre.

The Brothers Grimm, whose collection of folklore has left an indelible mark on literature, I am forever grateful. Your stories, with their rich tapestries of darkness and enchantment, have ignited the
imaginations of countless readers. They have provided the raw material for my exploration into the psychological and traumatic aspects of these tales, allowing me to delve into the depths of human experience.

Hans Christian Andersen, your fairy tales have touched the hearts of millions with their poignant themes of longing, transformation, and resilience. Your ability to weave tales of beauty and darkness has served as a guiding light for this project. Your stories have inspired me to delve into the psychological nuances of your characters, uncovering the hidden layers of trauma and resilience within their journeys.

Charles Perrault, your elegant retellings of classic fairy tales have enchanted readers for centuries. Your narratives have laid the groundwork for my exploration of the darker elements hidden beneath the surface. Your tales have challenged me to peel back the layers of innocence and discover the psychological depths that lie within.

The creators of the Arabian Nights, whose collection of tales has enchanted readers with its vibrant characters, captivating settings, and timeless wisdom. Your stories have expanded my understanding of the human experience, introducing me to new cultural perspectives and moral dilemmas. They have inspired me to delve into the psychological and traumatic aspects of these tales, exploring the universal themes that transcend time and culture.

To all of these incredible storytellers, I owe a debt of gratitude. Your tales have served as the foundation upon which I have built this reimagining of the fairy tale genre.

Your inspiration has guided me through the darkest corners of the human psyche, allowing me to delve into the psychological and traumatic aspects of these beloved stories.

I am forever indebted to your creativity, your imagination, and your ability to touch the hearts and minds of readers across generations. It is an honour to walk in the footsteps of such remarkable story-tellers and to contribute to the ongoing legacy of these timeless tales.

I would also like to thank the following bands that provided me with music during the write that enabled my mind to clear and focus on delving deeper into the psychological trauma that the characters survived during their experiences.

PowerWolf, Sabaton, Fury, Absolva, Iron Maiden, Within Temptation, Nightwish, Blackmores Knights, WASP. KISS, Control the Storm. (There are many more, but the list would be endless).

Like the story tellers of Old their passion of writing amazing lyrics and producing amazing music holds a deep personal and emotional connection with their fans, and for that I thank you and hope to see you on the road sometime again soon

To RACPA UK a heartfelt thankyou to the trusties and volunteers for the dedication that you give in helping victims become survivors

To my amazing Stepdaughter Stephanie, who had no idea I was writing this book, your strength helped me bring the stories to life. You are the proof that no matter what we experience in life, with friends and family you can overcome the hardest of situations.

To my father Nicholas (R.I.P) You showed me that no matter what life throws at you, it is the way that you receive and answer, you showed me Life and how to live. To be just a simple man with simple goals. To try and help others when they have fallen, and to honour and love your family.

To my amazing wife and soulmate Clare,
I dedicate this book to you with all my love

As I bring this book to completion, I want to take a moment to express my deepest gratitude and appreciation to you. Throughout this entire journey, you have been my unwavering source of support,
encouragement, and belief. I am forever grateful for your unwavering faith in me and for standing by my side as I embarked on this creative endeavour. Your belief in me, even during the moments of self-doubt and uncertainty, has been an anchor that kept me grounded.

Your words of encouragement, your gentle reminders of my abilities, and your un-wavering love have fuelled my determination to bring this book to life. I am forever grateful for your unwavering belief in me and for being my rock during the highs and lows of this creative process.

Your patience and understanding as I poured my heart and soul into these pages have meant the world to me. You provided the space and time I needed to fully immerse myself in the writing process, knowing that creating this book was a labour of love.

Your unwavering support, whether it was lending an ear to listen, providing feedback, or simply offering a comforting presence, has been invaluable. I am forever grateful for the countless sacrifices you have made along this journey.

Your belief in my dreams and the sacrifices you made to help me pursue them are testaments to your unwavering love and dedication.

You have been my muse, my confidante, and my greatest cheerleader.

Your belief in my abilities, even when I doubted myself, has been a guiding light that has propelled me forward.

Your unwavering sup-port has given me the strength to face the challenges that come with writing and publishing a book.

I want to thank you for always being there, for your love, your encouragement, and your unwavering belief in me and my dreams. This book is as much a testament to your support as it is to my own creative journey.

Your belief in me has allowed me to pursue this passion wholeheartedly, and I am eternally grateful for the love and support you have given me.

In the dimly lit corridors of our minds, there exist fragments of stories whispers of forgotten tales that have woven their way into the very fabric of our lives.

These tales, passed down through generations, have shaped our perceptions, beliefs, and fears. They have sparked our imagination, stirred our emotions, and left an indelible mark upon our souls.

But what if these stories were not just flights of fancy, but reflections of the darkest corners of our own existence?
In "Whispers of the Enchanting Dark: The Dark Secrets of Fairy Tales," we explore the profound connection between the tales we hold dear and the harsh realities of the human experience.

Through the timeless medium of fairy tales, we delve into the realms of psychological and physical trauma, unearthing the hidden truths that lie beneath the surface.
Each character within these stories bears the weight of their own personal torment and pain that mirrors the struggles we face in our own lives. From Little Red Riding Hood, haunted by the wolf's predatory gaze, to Cinderella, trapped in the clutches of an abusive stepmother, these characters embody the depths of psychological anguish and physical suffering.

The psychological trauma inflicted upon these characters is not merely an abstract concept, it is the very essence of their existence.

We witness the scars etched upon their souls, the shattered dreams, and the profound impact of their experiences.

These tales become windows into the human condition, illuminating the profound complexities of our minds and the indomitable spirit that can rise from the depths of despair.

But it is not only within the realm of fiction that these stories hold relevance. The dark secrets embedded within the tales are reflected in our own lives, offering a mirror through which we can confront our own demons. The psychological traumas explored within these pages resonate with our own experiences, reminding us of the fragility and resilience of the human spirit.

By shining a light on the psychological and physical traumas endured by the characters within these ta-les, we hope to spark conversations, foster empathy, and ignite a sense of shared understanding. Through the exploration of their struggles, we gain insight into our own capacity for healing, growth, and transformation.

"Whispers of the Enchanting Dark The Dark Secrets of Fairy Tales" serves as a bridge between the fantastical and the real, inviting readers to navigate the delicate balance between the two.

We delve deep into the stories that have enchanted and haunted us, weaving together the threads of imagination, psychology, and real-life experience.

In these pages, you will encounter the darkness that lurks within us all—the monsters that dwell in our shadows and the scars that mark our souls.

But within this darkness lies the potential for redemption, for the transformative power of resilience and the unyielding spirit of hope.

As you embark on this journey through "Whispers of the Enchanting Dark, The Dark Secrets of Fairy" Tales be prepared to confront the ghosts of your own traumas, to question the narratives that shape your world, and to discover the profound truths that can emerge from the depths of darkness.

Open your mind, embrace the stories that have endured through time, and allow the whispers to guide you into the enigmatic labyrinth of the human experience.

Welcome to the world of
"Whispers of the Enchanting Dark: The Dark Secrets of Fairy Tales,"
Where the boundaries between reality and imagination blur, and where the echoes of our shared traumas resonate. Prepare to be both unsettled and enlightened as we embark on this exploration of the human psyche, one tale at a time.

Whispers of the Enchanting Dark

ACT 1

Little Red (The Scarlet Guardian) (Original by Charles Perrault)
Snow White (Original by Jacob Ludwig Carl Grimm)
Cinderella (Original by Charles Perrault)
The Master Thief (Original by Wilhelm Grimm)
Rapunzel (Original by Jacob Ludwig Carl Grimm and Wilhelm Grimm)
The Pack of Ragamuffins (Original by Jacob Ludwig Carl Grimm and Wilhelm Grimm)
Rumpelstiltskin (Original by Jacob Ludwig Carl Grimm and Wilhelm Grimm)
The Wedding of Mrs. Fox (Original by Jacob Ludwig Carl Grimm and Wilhelm Grimm)
The True Bride (Original by Jacob Ludwig Carl Grimm and Wilhelm Grimm)
Death's Messengers (Original by Jacob Ludwig Carl Grimm and Wilhelm Grimm)

ACT 2

The WOLF AND THE SEVEN YOUNG KIDS (Original by Jacob Ludwig Carl Grimm and Wilhelm Grimm)
The Little MERMAID (Original by Hans Christian Andersen)
The Angel (Original by Hans Christian Andersen)
Eve's Various Children (Original by Hans Christian Andersen)
The Hut in the Forest (Original by Jacob Ludwig Carl Grimm and Wilhelm Grimm)
THE MOON (Original by Jacob Ludwig Carl Grimm and Wilhelm Grimm)
Sleeping Beauty (Little Briar Rose) (Original by Jacob Ludwig Carl Grimm and Wilhelm Grimm)
JABBERWOCKY (Original by Lewis Carrol)
Prologue to Looking Glass (Original by Lewis Carrol)
The Nightingale (Original by Hans Christian Andersen)

ACT 3

ACT 4

Now has come the point of no return
And I'm feeling fire, fill my veins
The torches starts to burn
And the quest is starting
It's up to you to be forgotten
Saddle the horses now
The mindless shall fear
When we all reappear to rise up

Credited to, Lyrics by Kai Hansen (Gamma Ray), Track Avalon

"Like a phoenix rising from the ashes, the human spirit has an extraordinary capacity to heal and transform after enduring the deepest wounds of psychological trauma. With time, patience, and self-compassion, we can reclaim our pow-er, rebuild our resilience and rewrite our story with strength and hope."

Quote by Angeless Watkins-Gallar

Whispers of the Enchanting Dark
Act 1

Little Red (The Scarlet Guardian)

Once upon a time, in a dark and eerie forest, there lived a young woman named Rosalind. She was known as "Little Red" by the villagers due to the crimson cloak she always wore, reminiscent of blood in the moonlight. Little Red had an adventurous spirit, often wandering deep into the forbidden woods,
disregarding the warnings of her worried grandmother.

One fateful day, when the autumn leaves painted the forest floor with hues of orange and red, Little Red received news that her grandmother had fallen ill.
Determined to care for her, she packed a basket of medicinal herbs and provisions and set off through the treacherous woods to her grandmother's cottage.

As she ventured deeper into the forest, a sinister presence seemed to envelop the surroundings. The air grew heavy, and the whispering trees twisted and contorted, their gnarled branches clawing at the sky.

Unbeknownst to Little Red, a dark entity lurked in the shadows, watching her every move. Suddenly, a raspy voice pierced the silence.

"Little Red, Little Red, where are you going?" called a voice that seemed to echo from every direction.

Little Red turned, her heart pounding in her chest, and spotted a pair of glowing eyes peering at her from behind the thicket. It was the Wolf, a creature rumoured to be a manifestation of evil itself.

Fear gripped Little Red, but she summoned her courage and replied,

"I am going to care for my sick grandmother, Wolf. It would be wise for you to leave me be." Her words were bold, but her voice betrayed a hint of trepidation.

The Wolf's wicked grin widened, revealing rows of sharp, yellowed teeth.

"Ah, but Little Red, your grandmother is no longer in need of your care. She has already succumbed to her illness," he sneered, relishing in the anguish that twisted across Little Red's face.

Rage and sorrow flooded Little Red's heart, fuelling her determination to confront the malevolent creature before her.

She clutched her basket tightly and stepped back, ready to defend herself. With every step, the forest grew darker, the shadows growing deeper and more menacing.

The Wolf lunged at Little Red, but she swiftly sidestepped his attack, her cloak billowing behind her like a bloody veil. She swung her basket, striking the Wolf's snout, causing him to howl in pain and frustration.

Determined not to succumb to the same fate as her grandmother, Little Red fought with all her might, her survival instincts guiding her every move. As the battle raged on, a glimmer of light appeared amidst the darkness.

The full moon broke through the dense canopy, casting an ethereal glow upon the scene.
Empowered by the moon's radiant energy, Little Red delivered a final blow, driving a stake into the Wolf's heart.

With a blood-curdling howl, the Wolf collapsed to the forest floor, vanquished by Little Red's unwavering bravery. The once menacing woods regained their tranquillity, and the whispers of the trees turned into gentle rustling leaves.

Exhausted but triumphant, Little Red made her way to her grandmother's cottage, where she discovered a diary hidden beneath her grandmother's bed. The diary revealed the chilling truth of an ancient curse that plagued their bloodline, turning the women of their family into unwitting sacrifices for the malevolent Wolf.
Between humanity and the supernatural. A brooding vampire with a tragic past, a reclusive witch with ancient knowledge, and a tormented werewolf seeking redemption—all united in their fight against the encroaching darkness.

Together, they uncovered a hidden truth, buried beneath layers of deception and forgotten lore.

The village had been built upon an ancient burial ground; its foundations entwined with the restless souls of those who had met tragic ends.

The malevolence that had tainted the land had attracted the very creatures that plagued their nightmares. The Scarlet Guardian and her newfound allies embarked on a perilous quest to break the curse that held their village captive.

They delved into forbidden rituals, determined to break the curse once and for all, Little Red vowed to carry on her grandmother's legacy and protect future generations from the Wolf's curse.

From that day forth, she became known as the "Scarlet Guardian," standing as a beacon of hope against the forces of darkness that threatened to consume their world.

With each passing year, the villagers retold the harrowing story of Little Red's encounter with the Wolf, passing it down from generation to generation.
They whispered cautionary tales by the fireside, warning children of the dangers that lurked in the shadows, the darkness that could hide behind a familiar face.

The Scarlet Guardian became a symbol of resilience and determination, an embodiment of the strength that lies within even the most fragile among us. Her crimson cloak, once a mark of innocence, now bore witness to the battles she had fought and the blood she had shed to protect her loved ones.

But the horrors did not end with the defeat of the Wolf.

No, they seeped into the very fabric of the village, tainting its soil with a lingering darkness.

Other creatures of the night emerged from the depths of the haunted forest, drawn by the scent of fear and the power that emanated from Little Red.

Vampires with eyes that glowed like fiery embers roamed the outskirts of the village, their fangs thirsting for the lifeblood of unsuspecting victims. Witches cackled in their secluded hovels, brewing potions that twisted the minds and bodies of those who dared to cross their paths. And a pack of werewolves, led by a merciless alpha, stalked the moonlit nights, leaving a trail of carnage in their wake.

As the Scarlet Guardian delved deeper into her mission, she encountered these monstrous beings, each more terrifying than the last. She formed unlikely alliances with those who, like her, straddled the line their deepest fears, and made unimaginable sacrifices

Along the way, they discovered that the power of love, sacrifice, and forgiveness could be the key to unlocking the village's salvation.

As the final battle unfolded, the haunted forest bore witness to an epic clash between light and dark-ness. Shadows danced amidst the moonlit trees as the Scarlet Guardian faced the ancient evil that had ensnared her bloodline for generations.

With each strike, she unleashed a torrent of raw magic, fuelled by her undying determination to protect the innocent.

In a climactic crescendo of power and sacrifice, the curse was broken, and the village was liberated from the clutches of darkness. The creatures that had once haunted their dreams retreated into the shadows; their reign of terror vanquished.

But the Scarlet Guardian's journey was far from over. As she stood on the threshold of a new era, she knew that the battle against darkness would continue. With her allies by her side, she pledged to defend the vulnerable, to stand as a beacon of hope in a world teetering on the edge of despair.

The legend of Little Red Riding Hood morphed into a chilling adult horror tale a reminder that even in the face of unspeakable horrors, there is a flicker of light that can guide us through the darkest nights. It teaches us that within each of us lies the power to confront our fears, to fight for what we believe in, and to emerge victorious, even when the odds seem insurmountable.

SNOW WHITE

Once upon a time, in a desolate and forgotten corner of the kingdom, where the shadows danced with Malevolence, and the air was thick with an eerie silence, there lived a young woman named Snow White.

She possessed an otherworldly beauty that enraptured all who gazed upon her—her alabaster skin seemed to glow ethereally, and her cascading ebony hair shone like a starless night sky. However, be-neath her innocent façade, Snow White harboured a darkness that consumed her soul.

Haunted by a tragic past, Snow White sought solace in the forbidden arts of witchcraft. Her desires and ambitions led her down a treacherous path of darkness, as she delved deeper into the forbidden mysteries, her heart growing colder and more distant with every incantation.

The villagers whispered in hushed tones of her wicked ways, for her actions had become the stuff of nightmares. But none dared to confront her, for they feared her malevolent power.

One stormy night, as the thunder roared with a vengeful fury and rain lashed against the windows like shards of glass, Snow White received an unexpected visitor.

Seven dwarves, renowned hunters known for their mysterious ways and resilience, arrived at her doorstep. They had heard the chilling tales of her dark arts and sought her aid in battling an ancient evil that had plagued their lands for centuries—a monstrous entity that fed on innocent souls and revelled in their torment.

Intrigued by the dwarves' tales of the cursed forest and the grotesque creatures that dwelled within its depths, Snow White felt a thrill coursing through her veins—a thirst for power and conquest that resonated with her darkened heart. She saw an opportunity not only to confront the abominations that roamed the cursed woods but also to prove her own formidable prowess in the realm of the arcane.

Donning her black cloak, her once innocent eyes gleaming with an unholy anticipation, Snow White set forth into the heart of darkness. The dwarves, though wary of her intentions, had no choice but to follow, for they believed that her knowledge of dark magic might be their only chance of survival.

As they journeyed deeper into the cursed woods, the air grew heavy with malevolence, and a sense of foreboding settled upon their shoulders like a suffocating shroud.

Twisted trees with gnarled branches reached out like skeletal hands, their twisted forms a testament to the wickedness that permeated the land.

The very ground beneath their feet seemed to writhe with a sinister energy, as if the cursed forest itself was alive, hungering for their demise.

Unbeknownst to Snow White, the dwarfs harboured a secret—one that would shatter the fragile trust she had placed in them.

They had sought her not only for her formidable powers but also as a sacrificial offering to appease the ancient evil that lurked in the shadows. Bound by an ancient pact forged in desperation, the dwarves had vowed to offer Snow White as the key to their salvation, betraying her trust in the process.

The moment of treachery came when they reached the heart of the cursed forest—a place where the very essence of evil seemed to pulse with a sinister rhythm. The dwarfs, their eyes glazed with malice and their hearts consumed by their own fear, formed a circle around Snow White, their twisted intentions hidden beneath false camaraderie.

The air crackled with tension and a sense of impending doom.

As the first dagger descended upon her, Snow White's eyes flickered with a surge of dark magic—a power that she had homed in secret, unbeknownst to the dwarves.

The world around them erupted into chaos as she unleashed her wrath upon the treacherous beings that had dared to deceive her. In a frenzied frenzy, Snow White channelled her potent sorcery, summoning the vengeful spirits of the cursed forest itself.

The twisted trees sprang to life, their branches coiling like serpents, constricting the dwarves' frail bodies, and crushing the life from their treacherous forms. The very earth trembled beneath the weight of their wickedness, as if nature itself sought to purge their corruption.

With the dwarves dispatched, Snow White stood amidst the carnage—a twisted union of darkness and vengeance.

Her once angelic beauty had transformed into a reflection of her tormented soul—a haunting visage of a malevolent queen, her eyes ablaze with an unholy fire that danced with the shadows. From that day forward, Snow White reigned over the cursed forest, her wicked powers growing stronger with each passing day.

Her name became a whispered curse among the villagers, who spoke of the monstrous queen that had once been their beloved princess. They shuttered their windows and barricaded their doors, fearful of the horrors that lurked within the depths of the enchanted woods.

And so, the tale of Snow White and the Seven Dwarves twisted into a chilling legend—a cautionary tale of the dangers that lie in the pursuit of power, the darkness that can consume even the purest of hearts, and the profound consequences that arise when treachery and deceit taint the bonds of trust.

In the shadows of that cursed forest, where nightmares reign supreme, Snow White's reign as the queen of darkness endured—a chilling reminder of the fine line between beauty and malevolence.

SNOW WHITE THE QUEEN OF DARKNESS

Cinderella

Once upon a time, in a realm shrouded in darkness and despair, where the echoes of forgotten dreams mingled with the chilling winds, there lived a young woman named Cinderella. Her life was a tapestry
woven with tragedy and hardship, far removed from the glimmering ballrooms and fairy tale endings that once filled her innocent imaginings.

As an orphan, she was subjected to a life of servitude, her days filled with backbreaking labour and endless torment.
Within the confines of her stepmother's decrepit manor, Cinderella became a spectre of sorrow, her spirit crushed under the weight of her cruel guardians' disdain.

Lady Anastasia and Lady Drusilla, her stepsisters, revelled in Cinderella's misery, finding pleasure in her suffering as they subjected her to incessant abuse and degradation.

The stepmother, a cold and ruthless woman, stood as the orchestrator of Cinderella's endless suffering, her eyes filled with a perverse satisfaction at the sight of her step-daughter's anguish.

But little did Cinderella know that beneath the surface of her bleak existence, forces far more sinister were at play.

The manor itself, tainted by the darkness that permeated the realm, held a malevolent presence—a malignant entity that fed on the despair and anguish of those trapped within its walls.

It whispered wicked whispers into the stepmother's ears, urging her to further torment Cinderella, to extinguish any remaining flicker of hope that burned within the young woman's heart.

One moonless night, as Cinderella toiled in the dimly lit kitchen, her weary body aching from relentless labour, a mysterious visitor emerged from the shadows.

A woman, veiled in a tattered cloak and emanating an aura of both power and sorrow, approached Cinderella with an offer that seemed too good to be true. She revealed herself as Lady Seraphina, an ancient sorceress whose own tragic past had led her down the path of dark magic.

With her voice laced with both sympathy and a hint of mischief, Lady Seraphina offered Cinderella a glimmer of hope—a chance to break free from the chains that bound her.

She possessed the power to grant Cinderella a single night of respite and liberation, an opportunity to attend a grand masquerade ball held in the depths of the cursed forest.

For one enchanted night, Cinderella would be transformed into the belle of the ball—a vision of elegance and grace. Intrigued by the prospect of escape, Cinderella's heart fluttered with a mixture of excitement and trepidation, and she agreed to Lady Seraphina's proposition without hesitation.

The night of the ball arrived, and Cinderella found herself standing before the grand entrance to the cursed forest, her heart pounding within her chest.

The path ahead was shrouded in an impenetrable darkness, the air heavy with an eerie silence. But fuelled by a newfound sense of courage, she stepped forward, determined to seize this chance for respite.

As she ventured deeper into the enchanted woods, the very fabric of reality seemed to shift and twist. Ghostly apparitions flitted among the trees, their mournful whispers filling the night air. Strange, luminescent flora bloomed, casting an ethereal glow that guided Cinderella on her path.

It was as if the forest itself recognized her plight, offering its support in this fragile dance with fate. Finally, she reached the grand masquerade ball, held in an ancient and dilapidated castle hidden within the heart of the cursed forest.

The grand hall, once resplendent with opulence and beauty, had fallen into disrepair, its former glory now a mere shadow of the past. Yet, in the dim light, Cinderella could still see remnants of its former magnificence—a faded reminder of a world she had only ever dreamed of.

As she stepped into the ballroom, her breath caught in her throat. The grand chandeliers, though tarnished and caked with dust, cast a delicate illumination upon the scene.

Mirrors lining the walls reflect-ed her image, multiplying her presence and transforming her into an ethereal being, a goddess of darkness and light. Whispers swept through the room as Cinderella captivated all who beheld her.

The attendees, a motley crew of lost souls and enchanting creatures, turned their gaze upon her, bewitched by her radiant beauty and the air of mystery that surrounded her.

Time seemed to stand still as she twirled and swayed to the haunting melodies that filled the air—a symphony of desire and longing.

But amidst the revelry and the enchantment, a sinister presence lurked in the shadows. Lady Seraphina, the sorceress who had granted Cinderella this one night of respite, had orchestrated the ball as a sinister trap.

Her true purpose was to feed on the essence of Cinderella's purity, to drain her innocence and vitality until nothing remained but a hollow shell. Unbeknownst to Cinderella, Lady Seraphina had struck a deal with the stepmother—a pact born out of shared malice and a desire for power.

In ex-change for Cinderella's life force, Lady Seraphina had promised the stepmother eternal youth and power, ensuring that their malevolence would endure through the ages.

As the night wore on, Cinderella's stepsisters, fuelled by envy and resentment, conspired to expose her identity.

Their jealousy twisted their hearts, leading them to conspire with Lady Seraphina. Together, they hatched a plan to shatter the illusion of Cinderella's new-found happiness, to tear away the fragile façade she had clung to so desperately.

With venomous tongues and malicious intent, the stepsisters unveiled Cinderella's humble origins to the gathered guests.

Their words dripped with scorn and mockery, piercing Cinderella's heart like daggers. The once beloved and radiant figure now stood exposed and vulnerable; her dreams crushed beneath the weight of their cruelty.

In that moment of despair, Lady Seraphina revealed herself, stepping forth from the shadows with a malevolent smile curling upon her lips. She unleashed her dark magic upon Cinderella, her sorcery transforming the fairy tale ballroom into a nightmarish realm of torment and suffering.

The revellers, once joyful and enamoured, turned into grotesque spectres, their faces contorted with malice and their bodies twisted with an insatiable hunger for pain.

But Cinderella, her spirit battered but unbroken, fought against the onslaught of darkness.

She refused to surrender to the fate that had been crafted for her. Summoning an inner strength, she never knew she possessed, she confronted Lady Seraphina with defiant resolve.

In a desperate battle for her very soul, Cinderella channelled her pain and anguish, using it as a weapon against the sorceress. With a surge of raw power, Cinderella shattered the sorceress's hold over the cursed ballroom.

The Spectre's dissipated into thin air; their malevolence banished by Cinderella's unwavering determination.

But the victory came at a terrible cost—Cinderella's once radiant heart had grown cold and indifferent, consumed by the darkness that had plagued her existence. From that day forward, Cinderella walked a path devoid of light.

She became the mistress of shadows, a figure feared and whispered about in hushed tones.

The stepmother, now cursed with eternal youth and bound to the sorceress's malevolence, became Cinderella's puppet, forever tormented by her choices.

Her tale became a chilling reminder of the price one pays for seeking solace in the embrace of darkness—a cautionary tale of lost innocence and the consequences of a fractured spirit.

In the depths of the cursed forest, where dreams turn to nightmares.

Cinderella's legacy lived on—a haunting testament to the tragic fate that awaited those who dared to challenge the boundaries of their existence.
Whispers of her presence echoed through the ages, a reminder to those who heard them of the dangers that lie in the pursuit of power and the cost of forsaking one's own light.

And as the generations passed, her name transformed from a symbol of hope into a cautionary Tale a chilling reminder that not all fairy tales end with a happily ever after

The Master Thief

In the heart of a forsaken city, where shadows danced with sinister glee and secrets whispered through the cobblestone streets, there lived a master thief known only as Lucius.

His name invoked fear and awe among both the common folk and the elite, for he was a phantom of darkness, a figure of legendary notoriety.
Lucius possessed a rare blend of unparalleled skill and audacious cunning. He prowled the city under the cloak of night, his every movement calculated and precise.

No lock could withstand his nimble fingers, no treasure remained beyond his reach. He revelled in the thrill of the chase, the exhilaration of outsmarting his victims and eluding the grasp of the law.

But as his reputation grew, so did the dark-ness within his soul. The thrill of theft was no longer enough to satiate his insatiable hunger for power and wealth. He craved something greater, something that would elevate him to a realm beyond mortal comprehension.

Rumours spread like wildfire through the underworld—a fabled artifact, known as the Dagger of Shadows, whispered to possess otherworldly abilities.

Legend had it that whoever possessed the dagger would gain dominion overshadows, becoming an unstoppable force of darkness.

It was said to be hidden deep within the labyrinthine catacombs beneath the city—an impenetrable maze of forgotten secrets and unspeakable horrors. Driven by his insatiable greed, Lucius embarked on a perilous quest to claim the Dagger of Shadows for himself.

Armed with his unparalleled skills and an unyielding determination, he ventured into the bowels of the catacombs—a descent into madness and darkness that would forever change him.

As he navigated the treacherous depths, the air grew heavy with malevolence, and the walls seemed to whisper ancient curses.

The catacombs were a twisted realm of lost souls and forgotten nightmares, a place where the boundaries between the living and the dead blurred.

But Lucius pressed on, driven by an unyielding desire for power.

Each step forward brought him deeper into the abyss, his mind haunted by phantoms of guilt and remorse.

The shadows, once his allies, now seemed to mock him, twisting, and contorting in grotesque forms.

Finally, he reached the chamber said to house the Dagger of Shadows. A dim, eerie light emanated from a pedestal, casting an ethereal glow upon the artifact. It pulsed with an otherworldly energy, promising untold power and wealth to its possessor.

Driven by a mixture of excitement and trepidation, Lucius reached out to claim the dagger. But as his hand closed around its hilt, a searing pain coursed through his veins.

The Dagger of Shadows had claimed him instead—a vessel for its dark magic, an embodiment of its insidious power.

With each passing day, Lucius's transformation grew more pronounced. His once nimble fingers, now twisted and claw-like, could no longer distinguish between friend and foe. The shadows, once his allies, now engulfed him, their suffocating embrace consuming his very essence.

His crimes grew more heinous, his lust for power insatiable.

The city became a playground for his sadistic games, as fear gripped the hearts of its inhabitants. The law, once a formidable obstacle, now cowered before the malevolence that had consumed Lucius.

But even in the depths of his darkness, a glimmer of humanity remained—a flickering ember of remorse and regret.

But the Dagger of Shadows held him firmly in its grip, a relentless master that would not release its slave. Lucius had become a puppet, dancing to the macabre tunes orchestrated by the malevolent arti-fact.

And so, the master thief's tale transformed into a harrowing chronicle of the cost of unbridled ambition and the seductive allure of power. His legacy, forever etched in the annals of the city's history, served as a chilling reminder that darkness begets darkness, and the pursuit of ultimate power often leads to one's own destruction.

But amidst the depths of his despair, a glimmer of hope flickered. Legends spoke of a ritual—a dangerous and treacherous path to redemption.

Lucius, consumed by a desire to break free from the Dagger's grip, set out on a new quest, seeking the knowledge and power to sever the bond that bound him.

His journey led him to the remote corners of the world, where ancient texts and mystic artifacts held the keys to his salvation. He encountered sages and mystics, each imparting fragments of wisdom and guidance.

He delved into forbidden rituals and dared to challenge the forces that had enslaved him.

Through countless trials and sacrifices, Lucius inched closer to his goal. He discovered that the Dagger of Shadows was not invincible; it had vulnerabilities of its own.

Legends spoke of a hidden chamber, a forgotten sanctuary where the dagger's power could be unravelled. Armed with newfound knowledge, Lucius returned to the catacombs beneath the city, his steps echoing through the eerie silence.

He navigated the treacherous labyrinth with newfound purpose, his determination burning brighter than ever before.
Finally, he stood before the hidden chamber—a realm untouched by time, cloaked in mystery and guarded by ancient wards.

With caution and reverence, Lucius entered, bracing himself for the final confrontation that would determine his fate.

The chamber pulsated with an otherworldly energy as he approached the pedestal where the Dagger of Shadows rested.

The air crackled with anticipation, as if the very fabric of reality held its breath. Lucius knew that this moment would define him—a final test of his will and his resolve.

With a surge of courage, he reached out, not to claim the dagger but to release it from his grasp.

He whispered ancient incantations, invoking the power of light to counter the darkness that had consumed him.

The chamber trembled, and the dagger quivered, recognizing the presence of its once loyal servant.

As the incantations reached their crescendo, a blinding light enveloped the chamber, banishing the shadows and shattering the bond between Lucius and the Dagger of Shadows.

In that moment of liberation, a wave of relief washed over him, a weight lifted from his soul. But the battle was not yet won. The chamber, once a sanctuary, became a battlefield—a clash of opposing forces, darkness and light locked in a cosmic struggle.

Lucius fought with all his might; his every fibre dedicated to overcoming the remnants of darkness that clung to him. Finally, as his strength waned and his spirit flickered, the light triumphed.

Lucius emerged from the chamber, forever changed but no longer enslaved. The city, once a playground for his malevolence, breathed a collective sigh of relief as the dark-ness lifted.

Lucius, now a shadow of his former self, retreated from the world he had once sought to conquer. He sought solace in the forgotten corners of the earth, devoting his existence to repentance and redemption.

His name became a whispered legend—a tale of a thief who dared to challenge the darkness, and against all odds, found the light.

And so, the master thief's tale, once destined for a tragic end, transformed into a saga of redemption and rebirth. Lucius, forever scarred by the darkness he had embraced, became a beacon of hope for those lost in their own battles against the shadows.

His story served as a testament that even in the darkest of nights, the flicker of a single candle can illuminate the path to redemption.

RAPUNZEL

Deep within the sprawling forest, shrouded in an eerie mist that seemed to seep into one's very soul, stood a towering structure—an ancient, decrepit tower.
It loomed over the surrounding landscape like a haunting Spectre, its crumbling walls whispering secrets of forgotten times.

This was the prison of Rapunzel—a tale far removed from its innocent origins, now transformed into a sinister horror story that would send chills down the spines of even the bravest souls.

Rapunzel, cursed by a vengeful witch with a heart as black as night, was trapped within the tower's confining walls for an eternity. Her once lustrous golden locks, now imbued with dark magic, possessed a life force of their own.

They slithered and twisted, intertwining with the shadows, a constant reminder of the malevolence that had befallen her.

The tower, a looming monolith of her suffering, served as a macabre symbol of her eternal imprisonment.

The townspeople whispered tales of Rapunzel's haunting song—a melody that echoed through the night, haunting the dreams of the unsuspecting and drawing them towards the tower's foreboding presence.

Legends spoke of a forbidden ritual, a way to break the curse and free Rapunzel from her perpetual torment, but none dared to venture near the tower, for it was said to be guarded by unspeakable horrors—creatures born of nightmares and fuelled by the very darkness that plagued Rapunzel's existence.

But one fateful night, a daring adventurer named Victor, driven by his insatiable curiosity and a thirst for both fame and the unravelling of mysteries, found himself unable to resist the allure of the tower's enigma.

Ignoring the warnings whispered among the villagers, he embarked on a treacherous journey, determined to face the terrors that awaited him within.

As Victor ventured deeper into the heart of the forest, the air grew heavy with an oppressive sense of foreboding. The once lush and vibrant landscape twisted and contorted, becoming a nightmarish realm where thorny vines coiled like serpents, waiting to ensnare unwary souls, and grotesque creatures slithered through the undergrowth with malevolent intent.

It was a place forgotten by time, where the line between reality and nightmares blurred, and the true horrors of the world thrived.

Undeterred by the encroaching darkness, Victor pressed on, his heart filled with a mixture of trepidation and determination. The path before him was treacherous, fraught with unseen perils, but he refused to let fear guide his steps.

He knew that the fate of Rapunzel and perhaps his own destiny hung in the balance. The tower, a monolithic sentinel of suffering, rose before him like a beast ready to claim its prey.

Its dilapidated walls whispered secrets long forgotten, as if the very stones themselves remembered the anguish that had unfolded within.

As Victor ascended the tower's winding staircase, the creaking of each step sent a chill down his spine, echoing the torment that had once permeated these halls. The chambers he encountered along the way were filled with a desolate emptiness a void that seemed to suck the light and hope from his soul.

The walls, once adorned with tapes-tries depicting tales of love and valour, now bore the marks of decay and despair.

The air was thick with the residue of suffering, and the weight of a curse that had twisted innocence into a vile mockery of itself. Finally, Victor reached the pinnacle of the tower the heart of the cursed prison.

The room, bathed in an ethereal glow that flickered and waned, seemed suspended in time, as if the very fabric of reality had frayed within its boundaries.

And there, in the centre of the room, stood Rapunzel a mere shadow of the innocent girl she once was. Her once vibrant eyes, windows to a soul that had known nothing but joy, were now hollow and haunted, reflecting the darkness that had consumed her.

Her voice, a chilling whisper that carried the weight of a thousand sorrows, sent shivers coursing through Victor's veins. The curse had transformed her into a vessel of malevolence, her very presence a beacon of terror.

The strands of Rapunzel's hair, once an object of envy and adoration, now writhed and squirmed like serpents seeking to ensnare Victor in their deadly embrace.

They moved with a life of their own, reaching out with a sinister purpose, eager to bind him to the same eternal suffering that had befallen Rapunzel herself.
But Victor, driven by his mission and unwilling to succumb to the suffocating grip of fear, presented the key to Rapunzel's salvation—a relic rumoured to hold the power to break the witch's curse and set her free.

With trembling hands, he approached Rapunzel, his heart pounding with a mixture of apprehension and determination.

As he held the relic aloft, a cataclysmic surge of energy rippled through the chamber. The very foundations of the tower trembled, cracks spiderwebbing across the aged stone, as the curse fought to maintain its grip on Rapunzel's tortured soul.

The strands of her hair thrashed and writhed with newfound fury, resisting the breaking of the curse, their malevolence a testament to the darkness that had corrupted them.

In a moment of desperation and unwavering resolve, Victor pressed forward, plunging the relic deep into Rapunzel's heart.
A bloodcurdling scream tore through the air, the very sound reverberating with centuries of pain and anguish.

The curse shattered, and the tower itself seemed to convulse, as if relieved to shed its burden of darkness.

Light flooded the chamber, banishing the shadows that had plagued it for far too long. Rapunzel emerged from the ruins of her prison, her features softened, and her eyes filled with a glimmer of gratitude.

The curse had been broken, and she was finally free. Yet, as Victor's eyes met hers, they both sensed a profound change—a lingering darkness that clung to their souls like a stain that refused to be cleansed.

They fled from the crumbling tower; its once ominous presence reduced to a heap of ruins. The echoes of its demise seemed to reverberate through the forest, a testament to the battles fought within its walls.

The world outside had changed, tainted by their encounter with the malevolent forces that had once held Rapunzel captive.

The shadows had seeped into their very beings, leaving an indelible mark on their spirits. And so, Rapunzel and Victor, forever bound by the darkness that had consumed them, embarked on a harrowing journey—a twisted odyssey that led them through a realm where nightmares bled into reality and malevolence lurked behind every corner.

They became warriors, vigilantes of the night, protectors of the innocent, fighting against the encroaching forces of evil that threatened to devour the world.

Their story, a chilling testament to the resilience of the human spirit and the unyielding power of love, served as a stark reminder that even in the face of unspeakable horrors, there is always a glimmer of hope—a beacon of light that can guide even the most tormented souls back from the brink.

Rapunzel's once enchanting tale had been twisted into a sprawling saga of darkness, resilience, and the unending battle between light and shadow.

And as they ventured forth into the unknown, the echoes of Rapunzel's haunting song lingered in the air, a haunting reminder of the horrors they had endured and the horrors that still awaited them.

RAPUNZEL'S REVENGE

THE PACK OF RAGAMUFFINS

Once upon a time, in a forgotten corner of a desolate village shrouded in eternal twilight, there lived a pack of Ragamuffins a group of children who roamed the streets, their tattered clothes blending seamlessly with the shadows that engulfed them.

They were outcasts, abandoned by society, left to fend for themselves in a world that had turned its back on them.

Legend whispered tales of their peculiar origin a curse that had befallen the village long ago. It was said that a vengeful sorceress, scorned by the townsfolk, cast a spell that transformed the innocent children into grotesque creatures.

Their faces twisted, their bodies contorted, they became a haunting sight to behold—a constant reminder of the town's sins and the darkness that dwelled within. No one dared venture near the pack of ragamuffins.
Their presence invoked a deep-rooted fear, as if they were harbingers of a malevolent force that lingered just beyond the edges of perception.

Yet, as the moon rose high in the night sky, whispers echoed through the village—a desperate plea for salvation, for the curse to be lifted.

It was on one fateful night, when the air was heavy with anticipation and the village shrouded in a dense fog that seemed to seep into the very souls of its inhabitants, that a brave traveller named Samuel stumbled upon the town.

Unaware of the dark secret that lurked within, he found himself drawn to the mysteries that lay hidden beneath the surface.

As Samuel wandered through the deserted streets, he couldn't help but notice the faint sound of laughter, echoing in the distance. Curiosity gnawed at his insides, compelling him to follow the haunting melody.

It led him deeper into the heart of the village, where the pack of ragamuffins awaited.

Their eyes, once filled with despair, now shimmered with a glimmer of hope as they beheld Samuel—a potential saviour who had unknowingly stumbled upon their path.

The leader of the pack, a child with eyes as dark as night and a voice that seemed to carry the weight of the world, stepped forward and revealed the truth of their existence.

Long ago, the sorceress had cursed them not out of malice, but as a desperate plea for redemption. The pack of ragamuffins reflected the town's forgotten sins, a collective embodiment of the darkness that had tainted their souls.

Only by breaking the curse and facing the horrors of their past could the village find absolution.

Samuel, filled with a mixture of trepidation and determination, vowed to aid the ragamuffins in their quest for redemption. Together, they embarked on a journey that would test their resilience, for the path to salvation was fraught with nightmarish trials and monstrous adversaries.

They ventured into the depths of the ancient forest, a place teeming with ancient spirits and malevolent creatures. Shadows danced among the gnarled trees, whispering secrets of forgotten evils.

The pack of ragamuffins, guided by their unwavering leader, confronted their darkest fears head-on, battling the demons that threatened to consume their very souls.

As they faced each trial, their appearances began to transform a reflection of their inner battles and the redemption they sought. Their twisted forms gradually shifted; their ragged clothes replaced by garments of purity.

The curse, now weakened by their collective resolve, started to unravel, and glimmers of their true selves emerged from the darkness that had enshrouded them for so long.

Finally, after a series of arduous tests, they reached the heart of the forest a forgotten shrine that held the key to their salvation. Within its depths, they confronted the embodiment of their collective sins an ancient entity born of the village's darkest secrets.

It was a battle that tested their resolve to the core, a battle that required them to confront the shadows that lurked within their own hearts.

With the combined strength of Samuel and the pack of ragamuffins, they triumphed over the malevolent entity, breaking the curse that had plagued them for so long.

The darkness that had consumed the village began to recede, replaced by a glimmer of light and the promise of redemption.

As the curse lifted, the pack of ragamuffins transformed into the children they once were innocence restored, their disfigured forms healed.

They were embraced by the villagers, who recognized the truth in their own culpability. The village, forever changed by the horrors they had faced, vowed to create a world free from the sins of their past, a world where no child would be forsaken or forgotten.

And so, the pack of ragamuffins became a symbol of resilience and redemption, a testament to the enduring power of hope and the capacity for change.

Their tale, a haunting parable of the darkness that dwells within us all, serves as a reminder that even in the most abhorrent circumstances, redemption and forgiveness can prevail, illuminating the path to a brighter future.

From that day forward, the village thrived, its people bound by a newfound sense of unity and compassion.

The pack of ragamuffins, no longer outcasts, found solace in the warmth of their community, forever cherishing the memories of their trials and the friendships forged in the crucible of darkness.

Their story echoed throughout the generations, a cautionary tale of the consequences of turning a blind eye to the suffering of others, of the importance of confronting our own demons, and the transformative power of empathy and acceptance.

And so, the legend of the pack of ragamuffins endured, a reminder to all who heard it that even in the darkest of times, there is always hope.
hope that can illuminate even the most shadowed corners of our souls.

RUMPELSTILTSKIN

Deep within the heart of the ancient forest, where time seemed to stand still, and the trees whispered ancient secrets, a malevolent presence lurked.

Rumpelstiltskin, a creature of darkness and cunning, held sway over the land, his insidious machinations woven into the fabric of the realm.

Legends spoke of his twisted desires, his insatiable hunger for power and control.

It was said that Rumpelstiltskin could spin straw into gold, a seemingly miraculous ability that drew the attention of those desperate enough to seek his aid.

But behind the façade of wealth and prosperity lay a sinister truth—a truth that few dared to acknowledge.

In a quaint village not far from the heart of the forest, a young woman named Amelia found herself ensnared in a web of misfortune.

Orphaned at a young age, she had struggled to survive, eking out a meagre existence in a world that seemed to conspire against her. Poverty and despair haunted her every step, driving her to the edge of desperation.

Whispers of Rumpelstiltskin's dark power reached her ears, igniting a flicker of hope within her weary heart. Tales of his ability to transform straw into gold filled her dreams, promising a way out of her dire circumstances.
With a heavy heart, she made her way to the heart of the forest, where she would make a pact that would forever alter the course of her life.

Amelia approached Rumpelstiltskin's dilapidated cottage, her pulse quickening with a mix of trepidation and desperation. The door creaked open, revealing a dimly lit chamber where the creature awaited her.
His hunched form and malevolent gaze sent shivers down her spine, but her desire for a better life outweighed her fear.

With a voice that dripped with an eerie charm, Rumpelstiltskin proposed a deal—a deal that would ensure Amelia's prosperity in exchange for something precious, something that would bind her to him forever.

He demanded her first-born child, an innocent soul to Mould and manipulate according to his whims.

Fear and uncertainty gripped Amelia's heart as she hesitated, torn be-tween the promise of a better life and the undeniable love she held for her unborn child.

The weight of her decision pressed upon her, threatening to suffocate her in a sea of moral turmoil.

In the end, desperation won over, and Amelia reluctantly agreed to Rumpelstiltskin's terms, sealing her fate with a whispered promise. The creature's twisted grin revealed his delight, knowing that he had ensnared yet another soul in his malevolent grasp.

Days turned into weeks, and weeks into months as Amelia's belly swelled with child. But as the day of reckoning drew near, an unexpected turn of events ignited a spark of rebellion within her.

She couldn't bear the thought of her innocent child falling prey to Rumpelstiltskin's dark designs.

In the darkest corners of the village, rumours spread of a hidden coven—a group of powerful witches who opposed Rumpelstiltskin's reign.

Their knowledge of ancient spells and forbidden rituals offered a glimmer of hope for Amelia's salvation. Amelia sought out the witches, their hidden sanctuary nestled deep within the forest, protected by enchantments, and cloaked in secrecy.

In the presence of these formidable women, she discovered a hidden truth—a prophecy foretelling the downfall of Rumpelstiltskin and the liberation of those ensnared by his wicked deals.

The witches revealed that Rumpelstiltskin's power stemmed from a cursed talisman—an enchanted amulet infused with the essence of darkness.

To break the insidious hold, he had over Amelia and her child, they must retrieve the amulet and harness its power for good.

With newfound determination coursing through her veins, Amelia embarked on a perilous quest, braving treacherous paths, and evading the minions of Rumpelstiltskin who sought to thwart her at every turn.

Along the way, she encountered allies in unexpected places—fellow victims of the creature's malevolence who had harboured their own secrets and desires for vengeance.

Together, they navigated through treacherous trials and overcame formidable obstacles, their collective strength growing with each step.

Their hearts burned with a fierce resolve to free themselves from the clutches of Rumpelstiltskin and restore balance to the land.

At long last, Amelia stood before the threshold of Rumpelstiltskin's domain—a realm suffused with darkness and despair.

With her allies at her side, she confronted the creature, their eyes locking in a battle of wills.

Amelia's voice rang out, filled with the power of the witches' incantations and the fire of her own determination. She demanded the release of her child, the breaking of their cursed pact, and the end of Rumpelstiltskin's reign of terror. The creature scoffed, his laughter echoing through the chamber.

He underestimated the strength that Amelia had found within herself, and the bond forged between her and her companions. They united, their combined magic and unwavering resolve creating a force that even Rumpelstiltskin couldn't withstand.

In a cataclysmic clash of light and dark, Amelia wrestled with Rumpelstiltskin, his power waning as her determination grew. With a final burst of energy, she seized the cursed amulet, wrenching it from his grasp.

A blinding explosion of light filled the chamber, consuming Rumpelstiltskin and banishing his malevolence from the realm. Amelia emerged victorious, the weight of her burden lifted, and her child freed from the clutches of darkness.

The village rejoiced at Rumpelstiltskin's downfall, celebrating Amelia as a symbol of triumph over adversity and the indomitable power of a mother's love.

From that day forward, tales of her bravery and the defeat of Rumpelstiltskin spread far and wide, in-spiring others to stand up against injustice and the seductive lure of dark forces.

Amelia and her child lived out their days in peace, the memory of their ordeal etched into their souls.

They became beacons of hope, reminding the world that even in the face of unimaginable horrors, the light of love and courage can prevail.

And so, the tale of Rumpelstiltskin serves as a chilling reminder of the dangers that lie within the shadows, the consequences of desperate choices, and the transformative power of bravery and sacrifice.

May we heed its warnings and remember the true cost of making deals with the darkness that lurks beneath our desires.

THE WEDDING OF MRS. FOX

Deep within the heart of the enchanted forest, where the moon cast an ethereal glow upon the ancient trees, a tale of darkness and deceit unfolded—a tale known as

"The Wedding of Mrs. Fox." This sinister fairy tale, shrouded in mystery and whispered among the villagers, held secrets that sent shivers down their spines.

Mrs. Fox, a captivating and alluring creature with flowing locks of fiery red hair and piercing green eyes, was no ordinary enchantress.

She possessed an otherworldly charm that bewitched all who gazed upon her, drawing them into her seductive web. Men and women alike fell under her spell, succumbing to her irresistible allure.

But beneath the veneer of beauty and desire lay a sinister purpose. Mrs. Fox's weddings were not celebrations of love but rather dark rituals, fuelled by ancient forces hungry for power and souls.

Unbeknownst to her victims, their union with Mrs. Fox would bind them to a life of eternal servitude, their souls forever entangled in a web of darkness.

Thomas, a young and impressionable man, had heard tales of Mrs. Fox's captivating beauty and the power she held over those who crossed her path. Intrigued and enthralled, he became consumed by a desire to possess her, to claim her as his own.

Driven by a reckless infatuation, Thomas ventured into the heart of the forest, oblivious to the horrors that awaited him.

As he neared Mrs. Fox's grand manor, an eerie stillness settled over the surroundings. The air grew thick with an unspoken warning, a silent plea for Thomas to turn back. But his longing, his obsession, propelled him forward, blinding him to the dangers that lurked in the shadows.

Entering the manor, Thomas found himself enveloped in a world of opulence and grandeur. Lavish decorations adorned the halls, and the scent of exotic flowers filled the air. The guests, dressed in their finest attire, chattered, and laughed, their faces flushed with anticipation.

Mrs. Fox, resplendent in her bridal gown, glided through the crowd with an air of regal grace.

Her enchanting presence commanded the attention of all, her gaze piercing their souls with an intoxicating mix of desire and danger. As the ceremony commenced, a sense of unease settled upon Thomas. Whispers reached his ears, tales of previous weddings and the fates of those who had become entangled in Mrs. Fox's web.

But his desire, his infatuation, clouded his judgment, making him blind to the warnings that echoed through the halls.
As the vows were exchanged, the atmosphere shifted, the air growing heavy with an unseen malevolence.

Gasps of horror filled the room as the guests' faces contorted, their features transforming into grotesque masks of terror.

The music, once enchanting, warped into a cacophony of discordant notes, sending chills down Thomas's spine.
He watched in horror as Mrs. Fox's true form was revealed—a creature of darkness and deceit, her beauty unravelling to expose the hideousness that lay beneath.

Her eyes glowed with an unnatural light, and her laughter turned into a haunting melody that echoed through the manor.

Frozen in fear, Thomas realized the true nature of Mrs. Fox's weddings. They were not celebrations of love but sacrificial ceremonies, offerings to appease the ancient forces she served. The victims, blinded by their desire for her, unwittingly became conduits for the darkness that lurked within her.

In that moment of revelation, a flicker of defiance ignited within Thomas's heart. He refused to become another pawn in Mrs. Fox's wicked game.

With every fibre of his being, he fought against the enchantment that threatened to ensnare him, summoning a strength he never knew he possessed.

Amidst the chaos and darkness, Thomas stumbled upon a small group of rebels—others who had man-aged to resist Mrs. Fox's allure, determined to break free from her clutches.

Together, they formed an alliance, united by their shared desire to expose Mrs. Fox's true nature and put an end to her reign of terror.

Through treacherous corridors and hidden passages, they navigated the labyrinthine manor, evading Mrs. Fox's minions who sought to protect their mistress at all costs.

Each step brought them closer to the heart of the darkness, to the source of Mrs. Fox's power.

At the heart of the manor, amidst the flickering candlelight and the suffocating presence of evil, Thom-as and his allies confronted Mrs. Fox.
Her eyes blazed with fury, her voice dripping with venom as she unleashed her power in a desperate attempt to subdue them.

But Thomas, fuelled by a newfound resilience, stood firm. He spoke words of truth and defiance, challenging Mrs. Fox's authority and exposing the insidious nature of her rituals.

With each word, her power waned, the ancient forces she had served recoiling in the face of his unyielding spirit.

A tempest of light and darkness erupted within the manor as Thomas and his allies battled against Mrs. Fox and her minions.

The clash of magic reverberated through the halls, shaking the very foundation of the manor.
With every strike, the darkness retreated, the grip of Mrs. Fox's power weakening.

In a final, cataclysmic confrontation, Thomas stood alone against Mrs. Fox, their eyes locked in a battle of wills.

He drew upon the strength of his allies, the love and determination burning within his heart, and unleashed a surge of pure light, banishing Mrs. Fox's darkness once and for all.

As the manor crumbled around them, Thomas emerged from the wreckage, battered, and bruised but victorious.

The forest, sensing the defeat of its malevolent resident, seemed to breathe a sigh of relief, its once-oppressive atmosphere lightening with newfound hope.

News of Thomas's triumph spread throughout the land, becoming a cautionary tale whispered among villagers.

The story of "The Wedding of Mrs. Fox" served as a chilling reminder of the dangers that lurk beneath the surface of desire and the consequences of succumbing to temptation without considering the true cost.

Thomas, forever changed by his encounter with Mrs. Fox, became a symbol of resilience and courage, a reminder to others to question the allure of beauty and to look beyond the surface.

His story, a testament to the triumph of light over darkness, echoed through the generations, reminding all who heard it of the hidden horrors that can lurk within the most captivating fairy tales.

THE TRUE BRIDE

Once upon a time, in a village plagued by an ancient curse, the chilling legend of "The True Bride"

whispered through the winds. The tale was shrouded in mystery, for its origins were rooted in darkness and despair. The villagers, burdened by the curse's haunting presence, feared the tale and guarded its secrets, shielding their children from the horrors that lay beneath its surface.

In this forsaken village, nestled in the heart of a desolate valley, lived a young woman named Elena. Her spirit burned with an unyielding determination to break free from the curse that had oppressed her people for countless generations.

While others whispered the fairy tale with trepidation, Elena delved deeper, seeking the truth that had been concealed for far too long. She poured over ancient manuscripts and tattered scrolls, piecing together fragments of the true story that lay behind "The True Bride." What she discovered shattered the illusions of romance and hope that the villagers had clung to.

The tale was not one of love and salvation, but a malevolent pact born from the depths of despair.

Elena learned that the curse had been forged by a sorceress, consumed by her own unrequited love. She sought solace in dark magic, determined to ensnare a mortal bride for the enigmatic Prince of Shadows—a figure of nightmarish power and insatiable hunger.

The true bride, chosen from the village's young women, would become forever trapped in a twisted union, her identity and freedom extinguished for the prince's nefarious purposes.

Driven by a fierce de-sire to break the chains of her people's suffering, Elena embarked on a perilous journey. The path be-fore her was fraught with peril, as the curse sought to ensnare and destroy anyone who dared to challenge its dominion.

Undeterred, Elena ventured into the heart of darkness, guided by an inner strength and a glimmer of hope that refused to be extinguished.

As she traversed treacherous landscapes and faced malevolent creatures, Elena encountered others who's lives had been irrevocably entwined with the curse.

They, too, sought to break free from its clutches, their collective pain and determination forging a bond of camaraderie and shared purpose. Together, they formed a fellowship, united in their quest to unravel the enigma of "The True Bride" and bring an end to the curse's tyranny.

Their journey took them through haunted forests, where twisted trees whispered ominous secrets and spirits of the dammed lurked in the shadows.

They faced riddles and trials set by ancient guardians; their every move scrutinized by unseen eyes. The challenges were designed to test their resolve and resilience, tempting them to succumb to the darkness that lurked within their own souls.

But Elena and her companions refused to surrender to despair. They unearthed forgotten relics and harnessed forgotten magics, each discovery bringing them closer to understanding the true nature of the curse.

Their shared experiences forged unbreakable bonds, as they drew strength from one another, even when the horrors of the journey threatened to tear them apart.

In the heart-stopping climax of their quest, Elena, and her companions arrived at the forbidden citadel of the Prince of Shadows. The castle loomed before them, a monument to despair, its malevolence radiating from every stone.

The true bride's chamber awaited, the place where the sacrifice was to be made, where the prince would claim his eternal companion.

As they ventured deeper into the castle's labyrinthine corridors, the weight of the curse pressed upon them, testing their fortitude.

Their footsteps echoed through the empty halls, mingling with the anguished whispers of past true brides who had fallen victim to the prince’s insatiable hunger.

Finally, they reached the chamber, a space suffused with an otherworldly gloom. The true bride, a young woman named Isabella, stood before them, her spirit weakened by years of torment.

Elena and her companions vowed to save Isabella, to break the curse that held her captive. With each step they took, the air grew heavier, the oppressive presence of the prince looming closer.

Shadows danced and twisted, taking on eerie shapes that whispered promises of power and immortality.

The true bride's fate hung in the balance as Elena prepared to confront the prince and shatter the curse once and for all. In a climactic clash of wills and magic, Elena faced the Prince of Shadows, their confrontation a collision of light and darkness.

She called upon her inner strength, channelling the resilience and hope of her people, while the prince unleashed his full, malevolent power. The clash reverberated through the chamber, shaking the very foundations of the castle.

Elena's heart pounded in her chest as she pushed back against the prince’s onslaught, fuelled by her unwavering determination to save Isabella and free her people from the curse's grip.

With each incantation, each surge of magic, she fought back against the prince’s darkness, summoning the ancient forces of light that had been long forgotten.

As the battle raged on, Elena's companions joined the fray, their own resolve bolstering her strength.

Together, they formed a barrier against the prince's influence, pushing him back, weakening his grip on Isabella's soul.

In a final, breath taking display of power, Elena unleashed a surge of pure light, piercing the prince's heart and shattering the curse's hold. Darkness recoiled, consumed by the brilliance of the light, and the prince's true form was revealed a broken and tormented being, stripped of his malevolence.

As the curse dissipated, Elena, Isabella, and their companions emerged from the chamber, the weight of centuries of suffering lifted from their shoulders.

The village rejoiced, their joy mingling with a sense of awe and relief. Elena, hailed as a saviour, became a symbol of hope and resilience, her name whispered with reverence.
In the aftermath of their triumph, Elena vowed to ensure that the truth behind "The True Bride" would never be forgotten.

She dedicated herself to the study of ancient lore and magic, becoming a guardian of knowledge and protector of her village. Through her teachings, the horrors and true hidden meaning of the fairy tale would be passed down through the generations, a cautionary tale to future children and a reminder of the strength of the human spirit in the face of darkness.

And so, the legend of Elena, the True Bride who defied fate, lived on a beacon of hope in a world where fairy tales could twist into nightmares.

The village, once haunted by the curse's grip, blossomed into a realm of resilience and renewal, forever transformed by the courage of one woman who refused to
surrender to the darkness that threatened to consume them all.

DEATH'S MESSENGERS

Deep in the heart of a forgotten forest, where the moonlight dared not penetrate, there lived a man named Victor.

He was a recluse, feared and shunned by the villagers who whispered tales of his involvement with dark magic and forbidden. rituals. Victor had long been fascinated by the mysteries of death, drawn to the macabre and the unknown.

One fateful night, as the shadows stretched long and the wind whispered secrets, Victor stumbled upon an ancient tome buried within the depths of his cluttered study.

Its weathered pages revealed an incantation, a powerful invocation that promised to summon Death's messengers—a group of spectral beings tasked with guiding the departed souls to the afterlife.

Intrigued and fuelled by his insatiable curiosity, Victor resolved to perform the ritual, for he yearned to glimpse the mysteries of the beyond.

In a moonlit clearing deep within the forest, Victor gathered the necessary ingredients—a vial of blood, a lock of his own hair, and a fragile glass orb said to possess a connection to the realm of the dead.

With trembling hands, he arranged the components, feeling a mixture of anticipation and trepidation. The air grew still, an eerie silence falling upon the clearing as Victor began the intricate incantation, his voice barely above a whisper.

As the final words left his lips, a palpable shift occurred in the atmosphere. The glass orb shattered with a resounding crack, releasing a burst of ethereal energy that danced and twirled in the night air. Shadows materialized, coalescing into ghostly figures with hollow eyes and tattered cloaks.

The messengers had answered Victor's call.

Their presence was chilling, their aura unmistakably touched by the otherworldly. The messengers glided forward, their ethereal forms aglow with an otherworldly light.

Each one bore the weight of countless souls they had shepherded to the afterlife, their expressions simultaneously serene and haunting.

The leader of the messengers, a figure draped in a flowing ebony cloak, stepped forward. His voice carried a timeless resonance as he spoke to Victor, revealing the purpose of their presence.

They were not merely conduits of death, but guardians of balance and order, entrusted with the delicate task of guiding souls between realms.

But as Victor continued to communicate with the messengers, he sensed a growing unease.

Their words turned cryptic and foreboding, hinting at a dark secret that lay at the heart of their existence.

They spoke of a hidden realm, a realm of unimaginable horrors where the souls of the wicked were condemned to eternal torment, their pleas for redemption falling on deaf ears.

Victor's fascination soon transformed into a deep-seated fear. The messengers' presence became suffocating, their aura tainted with an unsettling malevolence.

He realized that in his arrogance, he had unknowingly invited something far more sinister than he had bargained for. The messengers, in their duty to maintain balance, were not immune to the allure of power and the desire for control.

Night after night, the messengers infiltrated Victor's dreams, their hollow eyes piercing his soul. Their whispers grew louder, their words filled with menace and desperation.

They urged him to join them, to embrace the darkness that lurked beyond the veil of life. The line between reality and nightmare blurred, and Victor found himself teetering on the precipice of madness.

Desperate to free himself from the messengers' grip, Victor sought the guidance of an enigmatic sorceress known as Seraphina.

She was rumoured to possess knowledge of the ancient arts and had faced Death's messengers before.

Seraphina agreed to help Victor, warning him of the perilous path he had embarked upon.

Together, they delved into forgotten texts and conducted rituals to sever Victor's connection to the messengers. But with each attempt, the messengers fought back, their presence intensifying.

It became evident that they would stop at nothing to claim Victor's soul, to ensnare him in the very realm of horror they had spoken of.

As the battle between Victor, Seraphina, and the messengers raged on, the forest itself seemed to awaken, its trees twisting into grotesque forms and its shadows growing malevolent.

The very fabric of reality tore apart, revealing glimpses of the nightmarish realm that awaited them. The true nature of Death's messengers was revealed they were not impartial guides but malevolent entities seeking to corrupt and consume.

In a final, climactic confrontation, Victor faced the messengers head-on, his heart filled with a mixture of terror and determination.

Seraphina channelled her ancient magic, their combined strength becoming a beacon of defiance against the forces of death.

The battle was fierce and relentless, as the messengers unleashed their wrath upon the defiant duo.

Yet, fuelled by the desperation to reclaim his freedom, Victor fought with unyielding resolve. In a surge of willpower and magic, Victor severed the connection that bound him to Death's messengers, severing their hold on his soul.

The messengers shrieked in fury, their forms dissolving into wisps of smoke that vanished into the night. The forest, too, seemed to exhale a collective sigh of relief as the darkness receded.

Exhausted and shaken, Victor and Seraphina emerged from the forest, forever changed by their encounter with the other side. They knew that the horrors they had faced would haunt their nightmares for eternity, a reminder of the dangers of meddling with the realm of death.

Victor, now humbled by the harrowing experience, renounced his fascination with death, vowing to protect others from the perils that had befallen him.

Seraphina became his ally and mentor, passing down her ancient knowledge to future generations, ensuring that the story of Death's messengers would serve as a cautionary tale to those who dared to tread the path of forbidden magic.

And so, the tale of Victor, the man who dared to summon Death's messengers, echoed through the ages, a chilling reminder that some doors are best left unopened, and that the realm of death holds terrors that should never be awakened.

In the quiet of the night, whispers of their encounter still linger, a solemn warning to those who would dare to tempt fate and disturb the natural order of life and death

"Within the depths of darkness, lies the seed of resilience. With time, compassion, and self-discovery, we can mend the wounds of our past and find strength in our journey of recovery. The healing process may be challenging, but it is within our power to rise, to rewrite our story, and to reclaim the light that was stolen. Let your scars be a
testament to your triumph, for you are a survivor, resilient and capable of finding joy once again."

Quote by Angeless Watkins-Gallar

Whispers of the Enchanting Dark
Act 2

THE WOLF AND THE SEVEN YOUNG KIDS

Once upon a time, in a village shrouded in an eternal fog, there lived a mother goat and her seven young kids. This village, nestled deep within the heart of the haunted woods, was rumoured to be curs-ed, with whispers of dark forces and malevolent spirits that roamed its twisted paths. The mother goat, wise and cautious, raised her kids with tales of caution and the importance of staying within the safety of their humble cottage.

But fate had a different plan in store for them. Unbeknownst to the mother goat and her kids, a sinister presence had taken notice of their existence. It was a wolf a creature as old as time itself haunted by an insatiable hunger for innocence and an insidious desire to sow chaos and despair. Driven by his wicked desires, the wolf devised a diabolical scheme to lure the unsuspecting kids into his clutches.

He knew that their curious nature and thirst for adventure would eventually lead them astray, deep into the heart of the forbidding forest where he awaited.

ne gloomy morning, as the fog clung to the ground like a spectral shroud, the wolf set his plan into motion.

He disguised his voice, mimicking the tender tone of the mother goat, and called out to the kids from outside their cottage.

"My dear children, your mother has fallen ill and needs your help. Open the door and let me in, for I bring the medicine that will heal her."

The kids, their hearts filled with love and concern for their ailing mother, rushed to the door and swung it open without a second thought. To their horror, they found themselves face-to-face with the wolf a creature of darkness and death, disguised beneath a veneer of innocence.

Terror gripped their hearts as they realized the cruel trick that had been played upon them. But it was too late. The wolf pounced upon them, his jaws dripping with anticipation, his eyes burning with an unholy hunger.

One by one, he devoured the young kids, their cries of despair swallowed by the unforgiving forest. Yet, fate had a way of weaving unexpected threads of hope even in the bleakest of circumstances.

The youngest of the kids, a quick-witted and courageous soul, had managed to hide within a secret chamber beneath the cottage.

From there, the young kid witnessed the gruesome fate of their siblings, their innocence ripped away by the ravenous predator.

With grief and vengeance burning in their heart, the young kid emerged from their hiding place, determined to confront the wolf and avenge their fallen siblings.

The village, though plagued by the cursed fog and the sinister presence that lurked within, had not forgotten the tragedy that had befallen the family of goats. Whispers of the wolf's malevolence had spread like wildfire, and the villagers, though fearful, yearned for justice.

The young kid sought the aid of an enigmatic figure, an old hermit rumoured to possess ancient knowledge and secrets that could tip the scales in their Favour.

This hermit, wise and weathered by the horrors of the woods, shared with the young kid the legends and lore surrounding the wolf that had haunted their village for generations.

According to the hermit's tales, the wolf was no ordinary creature. He was a manifestation of the darkest desires and deepest fears that resided within the hearts of the villagers themselves.

The curse that plagued the village had given birth to this monstrous being, fuelling his insatiable appetite for innocence and driving him to perpetuate the cycle of terror.

Armed with this knowledge, the young kid embarked on a perilous journey to break the curse and bring an end to the wolf's reign of terror. They sought the aid of ancient guardians—beings of light and purity that dwelled within the heart of the woods.

These guardians, wise and ethereal, revealed the ritual that would sever the wolf's connection to the cursed village.
Guided by their unwavering determination, the young kid and the guardians ventured into the depths of the haunted woods.

The path was treacherous, filled with malevolent spirits and nightmarish creatures that sought to deter them. But the young kid's resolve remained unshakable, for they carried within them the hopes and dreams of their fallen siblings.

At the heart of the forest, bathed in an otherworldly glow, the young kid performed the ritual—an intricate dance of light and shadow, of sacrifice and redemption.

The veil of darkness that had shrouded the village began to lift, replaced by a faint glimmer of hope. The wolf, sensing his impending doom, launched a final assault, desperate to preserve the curse that had given him life.
But the young kid, emboldened by their newfound purpose, confronted the wolf with unyielding bravery.

They fought with all their might, matching the creature's ferocity blow for blow. The battle raged on, an epic clash between light and darkness, hope, and despair.

Finally, as dawn broke and its golden rays pierced through the haunted woods, the young kid delivered a decisive blow.

The wolf, its monstrous form wracked with pain and anguish, crumbled to the ground, its malevolent spirit dissolving into the ether.
The curse that had plagued the village was shattered, and the grip of darkness that had held them captive for so long began to loosen.

The villagers, once ensnared by fear and despair, emerged from their homes, blinking in the newfound light. They saw the young kid, standing triumphant over the defeated wolf—a beacon of courage and resilience.

Gratitude and reverence filled their hearts as they realized that the young kid had saved them from the clutches of their own fears.

From that day forward, the village honoured the memory of the brave young kid and their fallen sib-lings. They erected a monument in their honour a testament to their courage and sacrifice.

And the legend of the wolf and the seven young kids, a tale of horror and redemption, served as a cautionary reminder of the dangers that lay hidden within the hearts of even the most unsuspecting beings.

The village, though scarred by their harrowing ordeal, found solace in the knowledge that the wolf's reign of terror was finally at an end.

And as the years passed, the memory of the wolf and the bravery of the young kid faded into myth and folklore, a cautionary tale passed down from one generation to the next a reminder to never underestimate the darkness that lies within and the strength that can be found in the face of adversity.

And so, the story of the wolf and the seven young kids continued to resonate, a chilling testament to the resilience of the human spirit and the triumph of light over darkness.

The Little Mermaid

Once upon a time, in the depths of the unforgiving ocean, there lived a young mermaid named Marina.

Unlike her fellow merfolk, Marina was fascinated by the world above the water's surface—a world of beauty, mystery, and danger. Her heart yearned to explore the human realm, to experience the wonders that lay beyond her watery domain.

One moonlit night, as Marina swam near the surface, she caught a glimpse of a magnificent ship sailing across the dark expanse. Mesmerized by its grandeur, she couldn't tear her eyes away. But as she swam closer, a storm suddenly unleashed its fury upon the vessel, tearing it apart and sending the crew plunging into the tumultuous waves.

Driven by both curiosity and compassion, Marina dove deep into the churning waters, rescuing a young sailor named Erik from certain death.

She brought him to the safety of a hidden cave, her voiceless form captivated by his rugged beauty and kind eyes.

As Erik regained consciousness, Marina watched him with bated breath, desperate to communicate her gratitude. But her voiceless existence became a prison, her mermaid forms a cruel reminder of the impossibility of their love. Marina yearned to be with Erik, to share her world with him, and so she made a perilous decision.

Seeking out the enigmatic Sea Witch, Marina made a pact to gain a human form a form that would grant her the ability to speak and walk on land. The Sea Witch, with her sinister grin and dark magic, warned Marina of the price she must pay—a sacrifice that would forever change her life.

Marina agreed without hesitation, willingly trading her melodious voice for a pair of legs. As the transformation took place, she felt excruciating pain coursing through her body, her voice stolen away as if it were a mere trinket.

And so, Marina emerged from the sea, a human shell housing a silent soul. But the Sea Witch's twisted magic had unleashed more than Marina had bargained for. With every step she took on land, an insidious darkness crept into her veins, a hunger that gnawed at her very core.

The human realm, once a realm of wonder and possibility, revealed its true face a realm of vanity, greed, and merciless ambition.

Marina soon discovered that Erik, the man she had risked everything for, had fallen under the spell of a conniving enchantress named Morgana.

Morgana, with her seductive charm and wicked intentions, lured Erik into her clutches, ensnaring him in a web of deceit. Marina, her heart shattered, realized that she had become nothing more than a pawn in Morgana's twisted game.

Driven by anguish and a desire for revenge, Marina delved into the darkest depths of her newfound humanity. She tapped into the forbidden knowledge of the occult, seeking a way to break the enchantress's hold on Erik and reclaim the love that had been stolen from her.

With each step, Marina encountered horrifying creatures that dwelled in the shadows—the remnants of souls lost to despair and longing.

Their grotesque forms and haunting cries echoed through the corridors of her mind, a reminder of the cost of tampering with forbidden forces. Guided by her unyielding determination, Marina unearthed a forbidden ritual—a ritual that could break Morgana's spell, but at a terrible price.

She must sacrifice her own heart—the source of her love, her humanity, and her very essence. With each beat, her heart would grow colder, her connection to the world of emotions severed forever.

With heavy resolve, Marina embarked on her final quest. She confronted Morgana in a climactic battle, their powers clashing in a frenzy of magic and fury.

Marina's heart, now an icy vessel, radiated a power that surpassed the enchantress's darkest sorcery. In a final act of sacrifice and redemption, Marina cast herself into the abyss, plunging into the churning sea.

As her body merged once again with the vast expanse of water, her heart shattered into countless icy fragments, sealing away the darkness that had consumed her.

The spell was broken, and Erik awoke from his enchanted slumber, his mind no longer clouded by Morgana's influence. He realized the depth of Marina's sacrifice, the love that had driven her to such desperate measures.

But it was too late. Marina, the little mermaid who had yearned for a love that could never be, had become a tragic legend—a cautionary tale of the dangers of forbidden desires and the devastating consequences of tampering with the forces beyond our comprehension.

As the years passed, rumours began to circulate among the coastal villages of a ghostly figure that emerged from the sea during the full moon.

They spoke of a spectral woman with long, flowing hair and eyes that held both sadness and fury. Some claimed she lured unsuspecting sailors to their doom, exacting vengeance upon those who dared to betray love.

Whispers of Marina's existence spread like wildfire, her story becoming a cautionary tale told by fishermen and sailors huddled around their dimly lit taverns.

Superstitions grew, and seafarers would cross themselves and pray for protection whenever they spotted a glimmer of black hair in the sea.

But it wasn't just the sailors who fell victim to Marina's wrath. Fishermen who disrespected the bounty of the sea, plundering its resources without care or gratitude, faced their own horrors when their nets grew heavy with seaweed and decayed sea creatures instead of a rich harvest.

Their ships would become beacons of death, sinking into the depths with their wicked occupants trapped inside, forever condemned to wander the murky waters.

Marina became a vengeful force, a guardian of the ocean's balance, taking on a new form with each cycle of the moon. Sometimes she emerged as a monstrous creature, with scales and sharp teeth that tore through the hulls of ships.

Other times, she would appear as a seductive siren, her voice echoing through the night, luring men to their watery graves.
Her tale spread far and wide, reaching the ears of those who still dared to venture out to sea.

Mariners carried talismans, warding off the vengeful mermaid's wrath, hoping to avoid her piercing gaze and the icy touch of her hand. They left offerings at the edge of the shore, pleading for mercy and safe passage.

Marina's story became more than a cautionary tale—it became a haunting legend that echoed through the ages A reminder of the price paid for crossing boundaries, for seeking forbidden love, and for disrupting the delicate balance of nature.

To this day, as the moon casts its silvery glow upon the restless waves, those who are brave enough to sail the treacherous seas whisper of the ghostly figure that still haunts the depths.

Marina, the vengeful mermaid, forever cursed to guard her domain, serves as a chilling reminder of the consequences of defying the laws of the natural world.

Her story lives on, passed down from generation to generation, a tale of horror and warning that will continue to send shivers down the spines of those who dare to listen.

the Little Mermaid, in its twisted adult horror incarnation, serves as a chilling reminder of the sacrifices we make for love, the darkness that lurks beneath the surface of desire, and the price we pay when we stray too far from our own nature.

Marina's silent scream echoes through the depths of the ocean, a haunting melody that warns of the perils that lie hidden in the depths of our own hearts.

THE ANGEL

Once upon a time, in a world plagued by shadows and despair, there existed a young woman named Amelia. Fate had dealt her a cruel hand, leaving her orphaned and abandoned in a city that had long forgotten compassion and mercy. Her days were a relentless struggle, her nights haunted by the ghosts of a past she could not escape.

Amelia wandered the desolate streets, her steps echoing in the empty alleyways, as if the city itself recoiled from her presence. But amidst the bleakness, a glimmer of hope remained within her weary heart a longing for something greater, a yearning for a life free from suffering.

It was on a night steeped in sorrow and desperation that Amelia's world changed forever. As she sought refuge from the biting cold in a forgotten corner of the city, a radiant figure descended from the heavens.

It was an angel—an ethereal being of incomparable beauty, with wings that shimmered with an otherworldly glow.

The angel's presence enveloped Amelia in a warm embrace of serenity, and a voice, gentle yet commanding, echoed in her mind. It spoke of a hidden realm, a paradise beyond the reach of mortal eyes, where pain was but a distant memory and dreams transformed into reality.

Tempted by the angel's promises, Amelia pleaded for a chance to escape the harsh realities of her existence, to find solace in the paradise that beckoned.

The angel, with eyes that held the secrets of eternity, listened with a mix of compassion and caution before bestowing upon Amelia a single iridescent feather.

With a touch of its ethereal hand, the angel transformed the city around Amelia. The crumbling buildings dissolved into a landscape of breath-taking beauty—the once polluted air became a sweet symphony of scents, and the barren streets bloomed with vibrant flora.

Amelia found herself adorned in a gown of celestial fabric, her every step accompanied by the music of the heavens. At first, Amelia was captivated by the paradise bestowed upon her.

She revelled in the opulence, savouring the decadence that surrounded her. The angel's realm seemed like a respite from the relentless hardships of her former life a sanctuary where the wounds of her past could finally heal.

But as days turned into weeks, and weeks into months, the enchantment began to wane. The paradise that had promised eternal bliss revealed its sinister underbelly.

Behind the façade of beauty lay a web of darkness—a world governed by the whims of a capricious angel and tainted by its insatiable hunger for adoration.

Amelia soon discovered that the paradise came at a price—the price of her own soul. The angel demanded unwavering devotion, a surrender of her identity and will. Every desire, every whim, had to align with the angel's insidious agenda.

Freedom was but an illusion, and Amelia found herself a pris-oner once more, trapped in a gilded cage far more confining than her previous life on the streets.

The angel's paradise was a realm of paradoxes, where pleasure and pain coexisted, where joy was tainted by sorrow. Amelia witnessed the dark rituals performed by the angel's devoted followers, their twisted desires manifesting in unspeakable acts of violence and depravity.

The angel revelled in their suffering, feeding off their an-guish like a parasite. Haunted by the sinister truths she had uncovered, Amelia sought solace in the forbidden knowledge of fallen angels and ancient texts.

She discovered the stories of those who had fallen prey to the angel's seductive charm—once hopeful souls transformed into broken, empty vessels, forever tormented by the choices they had made.

Driven by a newfound determination, Amelia vowed to break free from the angel's grip and expose its true nature to the world. She sought out others who had dared to question the paradise's façade, gathering a small but resilient group of rebels who had glimpsed the truth beneath the angel's beguiling guise.

Together, they devised a plan to confront the fallen angel and sever its hold over their lives. Armed with the knowledge they had gleaned, they ventured deep into the heart of the angel's realm a realm where time stood still, where the laws of nature bent to the angel's will.

Their journey was perilous, fraught with traps and illusions designed to test their resolve. But Amelia and her allies pressed on, their determination unyielding. They navigated treacherous landscapes and faced nightmarish creatures born of the angel's darkest fantasies. Finally, they stood before the fallen angel, its once radiant form twisted and marred by its insatiable hunger for power. It sneered at them, its voice dripping with venom and arrogance, as it unleashed its wrath upon the rebels. But Amelia and her companions fought with a fury fuelled by the anguish they had endured, their will to to reclaim their lives unbreakable.

In a climactic battle between light and darkness, hope and despair, the rebels unleashed their collective strength, their spirits united in a resounding cry for freedom.

They channelled the very essence of their suffering, transforming it into a force that could rival the fallen angel's malevolence. With a final surge of power, Amelia struck the angel down, its celestial form disintegrating into ash.

The realm of paradise crumbled around them, revealing the bleak reality that lay beneath its seductive veneer.

Amelia and her allies emerged from the ruins, scarred but defiant. They carried with them the knowledge of the fallen angel's true nature, a testament to the dangers of surrendering oneself to false promises and the strength that can be found in embracing one's own struggles.

As they returned to the world they had left behind, Amelia knew her journey was far from over. The scars of her ordeal would forever mark her, a constant reminder of the darkness she had confronted and the resilience she had found within herself.

And so, the tale of The Angel serves as a chilling cautionary tale, a reminder that even the most divine can be tainted by corruption and that true liberation comes from within.

It warns of the seductive al-lure of illusions and the power of resilience in the face of overwhelming darkness.

In the annals of adult horror tales, The Angel stands as a testament to the strength of the human spirit and the enduring pursuit of freedom.

EVE'S VARIOUS CHILDREN

Once upon a time, in a desolate corner of the world, there existed a forgotten village named Eden Hollow. Hidden amidst the gnarled trees and tangled undergrowth, this village held a dark secret, a tale whispered only in hushed tones by the brave and foolhardy.

Legend had it that long ago, when the world was young and humanity took its first faltering steps, Eve, the mother of all mankind, gave birth to more than just Adam and his sons.

In the depths of the night, when the moon cast an eerie glow over the land, she birthed a brood of grotesque and monstrous creatures, known as "Eve's Various Children." These creatures, forsaken by their mother and shunned by humanity, were cursed to roam the earth, hidden from mortal sight. Each had its own terrifying form—a twisted amalgamation of man and beast, with features that defied the natural order.

They lived in the shadows, lurking in the dark recesses of the world, hungering for the taste of human flesh.

In Eden Hollow, the villagers lived in perpetual fear, for they knew that the children of Eve were drawn to their bloodline. The curse that had once given birth to these abominations now marked certain individuals, branding them as targets for the Children's insatiable hunger.

One such individual was Emily, a young woman who carried the burden of the cursed bloodline. Her life was one of constant vigilance, her nights filled with chilling nightmares of the Children's haunting visages.

The villagers whispered of the atrocities committed by the Children, tales of their merciless killings and gruesome feasts. Determined to break free from the curse and protect her village, Emily embarked on a treacherous quest.

Guided by ancient texts and cryptic prophecies, she sought out forbidden knowledge and sought alliances with powerful beings that dwelled in the darkest corners of existence.

As she delved deeper into the mysteries surrounding Eve's Various Children, Emily discovered a startling truth the Children were not simply mindless monsters.

They were pawns in a sinister game, manipulated by an ancient entity known as the Serpent, who sought to unleash chaos upon the world.

Armed with newfound knowledge and allies, Emily set out to confront the Children and the malevolent Serpent that controlled them. She ventured into forbidden realms and faced unspeakable horrors; her courage tested with each step she took.

The Children, sensing Emily's presence, emerged from their hidden sanctuaries, driven by an insatiable hunger that only her blood could satisfy.

They stalked her relentlessly, their eyes glinting with a hunger that mirrored their monstrous forms. Emily fought back with a fervour born of desperation, her every breath laced with the determination to end the curse that had plagued her bloodline for generations.

In a climactic battle between light and darkness, Emily faced the Serpent—a grotesque and twisted entity of unimaginable power. With her allies by her side, she engaged in a harrowing struggle, a clash of wills that would determine the fate of the cursed bloodline and the world itself.

As the final blow was struck and the Serpent's reign of terror came to an end, a profound silence descended upon Eden Hollow.

The Children, released from their curse, reverted to their true forms; fragile and vulnerable beings trapped in a cycle of suffering.

Emily, scarred but triumphant, emerged from the battle a changed woman. She had not only freed her village from the clutches of the cursed bloodline but had also unravelled the mysteries that had haunted her people for centuries.

With the curse seemingly lifted, Eden Hollow began to heal. The whispers of the Children's horrors faded into distant memory, replaced by tales of a brave heroine who defied fate and vanquished the forces of darkness.

But as the villagers celebrated their newfound freedom, a haunting question lingered was the curse truly broken, or would the Children's, legacy rise again, seeking vengeance for their stolen existence?

And so, the legend of Eve's Various Children remains etched in the shadows of Eden Hollow, a testament to the eternal struggle between light and darkness.

It serves as a chilling reminder that even the most sacred of origins can birth horrors beyond imagination and that the truest test of humanity lies not in our capacity for good, but in our ability to confront and conquer the darkness that dwells within us all.

Eve's Various Children stands as a harrowing journey through the depths of human fear, a cautionary tale that warns of the price of curiosity and the consequences of meddling with the forbidden.

It is a story of sacrifice, redemption, and the enduring strength of the human spirit in the face of unspeakable horrors.

THE HUT IN THE FOREST

Deep in the heart of a desolate and foreboding forest, shrouded in an eternal night, there stood a dilapidated hut, a wretched place known as the Hut in the Forest. Its existence was whispered in hushed tones, a tale that sent shivers down the spines of those who dared to speak of it.

It was said that the hut was cursed, a vessel of unspeakable horrors that lured unsuspecting souls into its clutches.

Legends told of a witch named Isolde who dwelled within the hut, a sorceress of unimaginable power and malevolence.

Her very presence cast a shadow over the surrounding woods, a darkness that seemed to seep into the very fabric of reality.

The villagers spoke of her vile rituals and twisted experiments, of her insatiable hunger for power and control.

One moonless night, a group of desperate travellers found themselves hopelessly lost in the forest. Exhausted and disoriented, they stumbled upon the Hut in the Forest, a sight that filled their hearts with both dread and a glimmer of hope.

Fear danced in their eyes as they peered through the dilapidated door, uncertainty gripping their souls.

Despite the warnings that echoed in their minds, the lure of refuge proved too strong to resist. With trembling hands, they pushed open the creaking door and stepped into the abyss of the hut's interior.

An eerie silence settled over them, broken only by the distant howl of the wind and the rustling of leaves.

Inside, the hut was a nightmare made real. The air was heavy with a stagnant mustiness, the stench of decay lingering in every corner. The walls, adorned with tattered tapestries and faded paintings, depict-ed scenes of unspeakable horror—creatures with twisted forms, demons of nightmares, and grotesque figures locked in eternal torment.

As the travellers ventured further into the labyrinthine hut, they were met with manifestations of their darkest fears.

Ghostly apparitions materialized before their eyes, taunting their minds with their deepest insecurities and regrets.

Whispers slithered through the darkness, carried on a chilling breeze, promising salvation, and damnation in the same breath.

Each corridor they traversed seemed to warp and twist, leading them deeper into a maddening maze of uncertainty.

The very architecture of the hut seemed alive, shifting, and contorting as if mocking their feeble attempts to escape its clutches. It became clear that the Hut in the Forest was more than just a physical structure—it was an embodiment of their deepest fears and darkest desires.

One by one, the travellers succumbed to the witch's insidious magic. Their spirits withered, their souls fragmented, as Isolde fed upon their fear and despair.

They became mere puppets, playthings in her sadistic game, their essence drained with each passing moment. Only one traveller remained unaffected by the witch's sorcery—the resilient and determined Amelia.

Her unwavering spirit and indomitable will shielded her from Isolde's grasp. With a fire burning in her eyes, Amelia vowed to uncover the truth be-hind the Hut in the Forest, to unravel the mystery that ensnared the souls of countless victims.

Driven by a fierce sense of justice, Amelia navigated the treacherous corridors, evading the witch's traps and illusions.

She unearthed fragments of forgotten knowledge, pieces of a macabre puzzle that revealed Isolde's origins—a tragic tale of betrayal, loss, and a thirst for power that had consumed her very soul.

Armed with the knowledge of Isolde's past, Amelia confronted the witch in a cataclysmic battle of wills and magic. Sparks flew, spells collided, and the air crackled with an otherworldly energy as they clashed, the very fabric of reality warping under their immense power.

Amelia, fuelled by her unyielding determination, unleashed a surge of ancient magic, a force so potent it sent shockwaves through the hut. Isolde, weakened and vulnerable, finally met her demise as Amelia's final spell shattered the witch's hold over the cursed dwelling.

With Isolde vanquished, the Hut in the Forest trembled and groaned, its sinister presence. dissipating like smoke.

The curse was broken, and the forest reclaimed its lost tranquillity. Amelia emerged from the remnants of the hut, her heart heavy with the weight of the battles fought within its walls.

But the horrors she had witnessed would forever haunt her dreams, a constant reminder of the darkness that lurked in the depths of the human psyche.

Amelia vowed to protect others from falling prey to the Hut in the Forest, to ensure that its vile secrets remained buried deep within the annals of history.

its malevolence lingered, a whispered warning to those who dare to wander too far into the heart of the unknown. For within the depths of every forest, a sliver of darkness remains, waiting to ensnare the unsuspecting souls who dare to challenge its grip on reality.

And so, the tale of the Hut in the Forest became a cautionary legend, a chilling reminder that even the most innocuous places can harbour unspeakable evil.

It serves as a testament to the strength of the human spirit, the power of resilience, and the unyielding will to confront the darkest recesses of the human soul.

THE MOON

Once upon a time, in a forgotten corner of the world, there was a village nestled deep within a dense forest. This village, shrouded in mystery and whispered tales, had an unsettling secret.

For every full moon that graced the night sky, the villagers would undergo a profound transformation—a transformation that brought forth their darkest desires and unleashed a malevolent force within them.

Legend had it that the Moon, an enigmatic entity, held dominion over the village, weaving its dark magic upon the souls of its inhabitants.

The curse bestowed upon them was an insidious one, for it brought forth their innermost fears, their most wicked cravings, and bound them in a never-ending cycle of torment.

Among the villagers was Luna, a young woman burdened with the weight of this cursed existence. She had witnessed the horrors that unfolded under the moonlit nights the once gentle townsfolk turning into ravenous beasts, tearing each other apart with an insatiable hunger for flesh and blood.

Luna had vowed to uncover the truth behind the curse and find a way to break its relentless grip on the village.

Driven by her determination, Luna delved into ancient tomes and sought out wise elders who held fragments of knowledge about the Moon's curse. As she pieced together the puzzle, a grim truth emerged—the Moon was not merely an observer but a malevolent force, delighting in the suffering it bestowed upon the villagers.

To break the curse, Luna would have to face the Moon itself. Armed with ancient rituals and forbidden magic, she gathered a small group of brave souls who shared her desire for liberation.

Together, they embarked on a perilous journey to reach the Moon's domain—an ethereal realm of shadows and shifting illusions.

As Luna and her companions ventured deeper into the Moon's realm, they encountered grotesque creatures born of nightmares, twisted manifestations of the villagers' darkest fears.

Each step forward required them to confront their own inner demons, fighting against the seductive allure of their deepest, most forbidden desires.

The air grew thick with tension as they approached the heart of the Moon's realm. Eerie whispers echoed through the corridors of darkness, their words laced with both allure and menace.

Luna's heart raced, her every instinct warning her of the treacherous nature of their quest. But she pressed on, fuelled by her unwavering determination to free her village from the Moon's curse.

Finally, they reached the heart of the Moon's realm a desolate landscape where the Moon, a sinister and ethereal presence, awaited their arrival.

Its pale light cast an eerie glow upon the surroundings, revealing the twisted nature of its power. Luna, fuelled by a mixture of fear and determination, confront-ed the Moon, demanding an end to the curse that had plagued her village for generations.

The Moon, sensing Luna’s defiance unleashed its fury upon her and her companions. Shadows writhed and twisted, taking on monstrous forms that sought to devour their souls.

Luna's group fought valiantly, their strength and unity pushing back against the overwhelming darkness. In a climactic battle between light and shadow, Luna, armed with a relic of ancient power, channelled her inner strength and unleashed a surge of pure energy against the Moon.

The realm quaked and trembled, the Moon's malevolent power faltering in the face of Luna's unwavering determination.

With a final burst of energy, Luna shattered the Moon's hold over the village. Its influence waned, the curse dissipating like a lingering mist.

The villagers, freed from the chains of their monstrous transformations, woke from their cursed slumber, their memories clouded with fragments of the horrors they had committed.

As Luna and her companions returned to the village, they were hailed as heroes, the saviours who had broken the Moon's curse. The village, now bathed in the gentle light of the moon, began to rebuild, and heal.

Luna, forever marked by her journey, became a guiding light for her people, ensuring that the Moon's curse would never haunt their lives again.

But Luna knew that the struggle against darkness was an ongoing battle. She remained ever vigilant, training new generations to confront the shadows that lurked within themselves.

The Moon's curse, once a suffocating shroud over the village, became a catalyst for growth, resilience, and the unyielding pursuit of light.

And so, the tale of The Moon stands as a testament to the indomitable spirit of humanity, the capacity to confront and overcome even the most malevolent of forces.

It serves as a cautionary tale, a reminder of the dangers that lie in succumbing to one's deepest fears and desires.

The Moon's curse, once a haunting presence, became a catalyst for strength and unity, transforming the villagers into a beacon of hope and unwavering resolve.

SLEEPING BEAUTY (LITTLE BRIAR ROSE)

Once upon a time, in a kingdom shrouded in an eternal night, a curse of unspeakable horror befell the land. Morgana, a sorceress consumed by her own twisted desires, sought to unleash a reign of terror upon the realm of Ebonia.

With her wicked powers and a heart corrupted by darkness, she devised a malevolent spell that would plunge the entire kingdom into an unending nightmare.

At the heart of Morgana's curse lay Princess Aurora, a young maiden of incomparable beauty and innocence. On the eve of her sixteenth birthday, the fateful night when the curse would be enacted, the kingdom was thrown into chaos.

As the clock struck midnight, a miasma of malevolence swept through the land, tainting every corner with an indescribable dread. The once vibrant and lively streets turned desolate, the joyous laughter of its inhabitants replaced with haunting echoes of anguish.

Aurora, ensnared in Morgana's trap, fell into a deep slumber, her life force tethered to the darkest recesses of her mind.

The curse had a chilling effect on the entire kingdom, transforming the once picturesque landscape into a haunting realm of nightmares.

The moon, once a beacon of gentle light, now cast a sinister glow that illuminated twisted and contorted shadows lurking at every corner.

During this harrowing darkness, a lone figure emerged. Seraphina, a mysterious sorceress feared by many, was drawn to the kingdom by a relentless pursuit of forbidden knowledge.

Rumours whispered of her ability to traverse the ethereal realm of nightmares; an expertise that made her uniquely suited to face the horrors that plagued Ebonia.

Guided by an ancient prophecy, Seraphina ventured into the depths of the cursed kingdom. She traversed treacherous forests where gnarled branches reached out like skeletal hands, and the wind carried whispers of despair.

The land itself seemed to shift and contort; an ever-changing labyrinth designed to ensnare the unwary traveller. As Seraphina delved deeper into the heart of darkness, she encountered twisted manifestations of the kingdom's fears and nightmares.

Grotesque creatures with mangled limbs and glowing eyes stalked the shadows, their feral snarls sending shivers down her spine.

She fought tooth and nail, her magic crackling through the air, as she confronted the grotesque remnants of the once innocent and beloved inhabitants.

But the horrors did not end there. The realm of dreams itself seemed to rebel against Seraphina's presence.

Illusions and mirages taunted her at every turn, distorting reality and clouding her judgment. Her mind became a battlefield, as visions of her deepest fears and regrets threatened to consume her. Yet, she persisted, drawing strength from her indomitable will and unyielding determination.

In her search for a way to break the curse, Seraphina encountered a reclusive sage known as Eldritch, a being said to possess ancient wisdom and knowledge of the arcane arts. Eldritch's lair was hidden deep within a foreboding mountain, where twisted spires reached toward the heavens like bony fingers.

The sage's gaunt face and hollow eyes betrayed the toll of his long existence, his voice a haunting whisper that spoke of forgotten truths and unspeakable secrets.

Under Eldritch's guidance, Seraphina delved into forbidden rituals and ancient texts, unearthing dark secrets that tested her moral compass. She learned of the curse's origins, rooted in a blood pact forged in desperation and anguish.

Morgana's lust for power had led her to strike a deal with an ancient and malevolent entity, sacrificing her own humanity in exchange for the curse's devastating power.

Armed with this knowledge, Seraphina understood the gravity of her task.

To break the curse and free Aurora from her eternal slumber, she would need to confront Morgana herself, severing the sorceress's connection to the dark entity that fuelled her wickedness.

The final confrontation between Seraphina and Morgana was a cataclysmic clash of sorcery and will-power. The air crackled with energy as they unleashed their most potent spells, their magic tearing through the fabric of reality.

The citadel trembled, its darkened corridors echoing with screams of torment and the anguished cries of forgotten souls. In a moment of desperation, Morgana unleashed a forbidden spell, drawing upon the very essence of the cursed land.

Shadows converged around her, forming a monstrous entity of darkness and malice. Seraphina, fuelled by her unwavering resolve and the love she held for the kingdom she sought to save, unleashed a blinding surge of light that pierced through the darkness, shattering the abomination.

The spell, broken by the clash of opposing forces, ripped through the cursed kingdom like a shockwave, dispelling the nightmare that had plagued Ebonia for far too long. Aurora, freed from her slumber, awoke to a world reborn a realm basking in the warm embrace of dawn, its scars healing under the soothing touch of Seraphina's magic.

As the sun rose over the kingdom, its golden rays kissed the land, illuminating the faces of its grateful inhabitants. Aurora, hailed as the saviour of Ebonia, ascended to the throne, her reign marked by an era of unity and prosperity.

Seraphina, forever changed by her harrowing journey, retreated into the shadows, a silent guardian ready to confront any remnants of dark-ness that dared to resurface.

But even as peace settled over the land, whispers persisted of Morgana's lingering presence, a spectral reminder that evil, once unleashed, can never truly be eradicated. Seraphina, forever haunted by the horrors she witnessed, knew that her battle against darkness was far from over.

She vowed to remain vigilant, an eternal sentinel standing between the realm of nightmares and the fragile peace that had been won.

As Aurora settled into her newfound role as queen, the remnants of Morgana's curse continued to cast a shadow over the kingdom. The once jubilant townsfolk, plagued by restless nights and haunting visions, found themselves trapped in a twisted realm between sleep and wakefulness.

Nightmares tormented their every step, manifesting as ethereal creatures that lurked in the darkest corners of their minds. Desperate for a solution, Queen Aurora sought the aid of Seraphina once more.

The sorceress, now a recluse haunted by her own battles with darkness, hesitated to confront the malevolence that had lingered even after Morgana's defeat.

Reluctantly, she agreed to delve into the depths of the nightmare realm to uncover the source of the lingering curse.

Together, Queen Aurora and Seraphina embarked on a treacherous journey through the realm of dreams a realm where reality twisted and contorted into grotesque shapes, and the boundaries of sanity blurred.

Nightmarish landscapes greeted their every step, filled with twisted trees, wailing spirits, and unsettling echoes. As they ventured deeper, they discovered a malevolent entity lurking in the heart of the nightmare realm.

It was the embodiment of Morgana's lingering darkness, a manifestation of her unfulfilled desires and twisted ambitions. This entity, known as the Shadow Queen, fed off the fear and despair of the kingdom, perpetuating the curse and ensnaring souls in its icy grip.

To confront the Shadow Queen, Queen Aurora and Seraphina had to navigate a treacherous labyrinth of illusions and psychological torment.

The realm twisted their deepest fears into grotesque manifestations, forcing them to confront their own inner demons.

They braved hallucinations that tore at their very essence, threatening to unravel their sanity.

At the climax of their journey, Queen Aurora faced the Shadow Queen in a battle that would determine the fate of the kingdom. Seraphina, drawing upon the remnants of her own shattered past, channelled her inner strength to bolster Aurora's resolve.

Together, they unleashed a torrent of light and magic, hoping to banish the darkness once and for all.

But the Shadow Queen, fuelled by the collective nightmares of the kingdom, proved to be a formidable foe. Its tendrils of darkness snaked through the air, suffocating the light, and threatening to consume all hope.

Queen Aurora, realizing that victory required a sacrifice, made the ultimate choice.

She willingly offered herself as a vessel for the darkness, allowing the Shadow Queen to possess her.

In a moment of darkness and despair, the realm shook with the force of the sacrifice.

The Shadow Queen, now trapped within Aurora's physical form, found itself at the mercy of a pure-hearted soul.

Aurora, guided by her unwavering love for her kingdom, fought to regain control, refusing to let the darkness consume her entirely.

With every ounce of her strength, Aurora managed to reclaim her body and cast the Shadow Queen out. The nightmare realm collapsed upon itself, leaving behind only remnants of the curse that once plagued Ebonia.

The kingdom, free from the clutches of darkness, began to heal.

However, the battle had taken its toll on Aurora. The lingering effects of the possession had left her marked with an eternal darkness a constant reminder of the sacrifices made to save the kingdom.

The people, forever grateful for their queen's bravery, embraced her as a symbol of resilience and strength. As Aurora ruled with wisdom and compassion, she never forgot the horrors she had faced.

She established an order of Dreamweaver’s, individuals with the ability to navigate the realm of dreams and protect the kingdom from future threats.

Seraphina, now a mentor to the Dreamweaver’s, shared her knowledge and guided the new generation in their fight against the darkness that still whispered in the shadows.

And so, the tale of Sleeping Beauty, in its expanded adult horror rendition, serves as a testament to the enduring power of love and sacrifice in the face of unspeakable darkness.

It reminds us that even after a battle is won, the scars of the past remain, serving as a constant reminder of the eternal struggle between light and shadow.

Sleeping Beauty stands as a chilling re-minder of the strength and resilience that can be found within us when faced with the darkest of nightmares.

JABBERWOCKY

Deep within the heart of a forgotten realm, where nightmares loom and darkness reigns supreme, a tale of unimaginable terror unfolds the legend of Jabberwocky.

This retelling delves even deeper into the twisted horrors that lurk within its twisted depths. Brace yourself for an extreme adult horror story that will push the boundaries of your sanity.

In a village cloaked in perpetual darkness, Emilia, a young woman tormented by visions of the Jabberwocky, found herself trapped in a waking nightmare.

The grotesque creature's presence haunted her every thought, its malevolence threatening to consume her soul.

Determined to uncover the truth and confront her tormentor, Emilia embarked on a treacherous journey through the darkest recesses of her mind.

As she delved deeper into the forbidden realms, Emilia's descent into madness mirrored the monstrous entity that plagued her existence.

The lines between reality and illusion blurred, and she found herself entangled in a web of macabre rituals and unholy practices. The whispers of the Jabberwocky's devo-tees lured her further into the abyss, their promises of power and pleasure tempting her fragile psyche.

Under the Jabberwocky's command, Emilia's depravity knew no bounds.

She became the embodiment of fear, her every step leaving a trail of broken souls and shattered lives. The village, once a bastion of hope, now lay in ruins, its inhabitants reduced to trembling shells of their former selves.

Within the depraved cult's secret lair, Emilia bore witness to unspeakable acts of cruelty and sadism. The air reeked of blood and decay, mingling with the frenzied cries of the cultists.

They revelled in the terror they inflicted upon one another, their bodies adorned with grotesque markings, a testament to their unholy devotion.

Emilia, seduced by the intoxicating allure of forbidden knowledge, became an active participant in the cult's grotesque rituals.

Her soul tainted by darkness; she revelled in the perverse delights offered by her fellow worshippers.

They danced in frenzied ecstasy, their bodies intertwined in a grotesque ballet of violence and desire.

Emilia's victims were subjected to unspeakable tortures, their agonized screams echoing through the desolate streets. She revelled in their suffering, relishing the terror that danced in their eyes before snuffing out their lives.

The very air seemed to thicken with the stench of decay, as the Jabberwocky's influence twisted reality into a grotesque nightmare.

As her desires spiralled out of control, Emilia's transformation into a vessel of the Jabberwocky's malevolence became evident.

The once timid and tormented woman now embraced her role as an agent of chaos, spreading fear and suffering wherever she treads. Her victims, both innocent and guilty, fell prey to her insatiable hunger for power and pain.

The moon hung heavy in the sky, casting an eerie glow upon the twisted tableau of horror.

Emilia, clad in tattered garments stained with the blood of her victims, danced under its pale light, her movements a perverse celebration of the grotesque.

Each step resonated with the cries of the tormented souls she had claimed, the very ground trembling in response to her malevolent power.

In the heart of the village, they faced the embodiment of their nightmares the Jabberwocky itself.

Towering above them, its monstrous form twisted and distorted, the creature exuded an aura of pure malevolence. Its fangs glistened with the blood of its victims, and its eyes burned with a sickening hunger.

But amidst the grotesque carnival of horrors, a glimmer of hope emerged an enigmatic figure known as the Shadow Weaver.

Rumoured to possess the knowledge to unbind the Jabberwocky's influence, the Shadow Weaver offered Emilia a chance at redemption a slim ray of light in the suffocating darkness.

Emilia, torn between her insatiable thirst for power and the flickering ember of her humanity, made a fateful decision.

She turned against her fellow cultists; their once-devoted allies transformed into grotesque monstrosities under the Jabberwocky's dominion.

With each life she claimed, the creature's grip on reality weakened, its power slowly unravelling.

A fierce battle ensued, the clash of steel against flesh reverberating through the night. The survivors fought with a ferocity born of desperation, their souls aflame with the need to vanquish the horrors that had plagued their existence.

But the Jabberwocky proved a formidable adversary, its monstrous power overwhelming their resolve.

One by one, the survivors fell, their bodies broken, and spirits shattered.

Emilia, once a tortured victim herself, now revelled in the chaos she had unleashed. She danced among the fallen, her laughter a chilling melody that echoed through the night.

The survivors' valiant efforts had been in vain—their dreams of liberation crushed under the weight of the Jabberwocky's cruelty.

n a final, cataclysmic confrontation, Emilia stood face to face with the Jabberwocky an abomination of flesh and nightmares, its presence suffocating the very air around her.

Bloodlust burned in her eyes as she unleashed her fury upon the creature, her weapon slashing through sinew and bone.

As the moon reached its zenith, bathing the village in an ethereal glow, Emilia stood triumphant amid the carnage.

The once beautiful village now lay in ruins, its inhabitants lost to the darkness.

The Jabberwocky's influence had claimed them all, leaving nothing but a wasteland of despair.

But victory came at a price. As the creature's life force drained away, Emilia found herself alone felling her own humanity slip further into the abyss.

She had become a monster, stained by the horrors she had witnessed and committed. The realization of her monstrous transformation finally sank in, and a shiver ran down her spine.

She had become the very embodiment of the nightmare she had fought against—an agent of chaos and destruction. Haunted by her own reflection, Emilia roamed the desolate village, the weight of her actions pressing heavily upon her soul.

The moon, a silent witness to her descent into madness, bathed her in its cold light, a constant reminder of the horrors she had unleashed.

And so, dear reader, as the moon wanes and darkness recedes, let this tale serve as a chilling reminder of the fragility of our humanity.

The legend of the Jabberwocky, with its extended tale of terror, cautions against the seductive lure of power and the devastating consequences of surrendering to our darkest desires. For when we embrace the darkness within, we risk losing ourselves entirely, consumed by the very horrors we sought to conquer.

Prologue to Looking Glass

Deep in the recesses of the human psyche lies a realm untouched by reason or sanity; a place where nightmares manifest and reality warps into grotesque visions.

It is within this treacherous landscape that the Prologue to Looking Glass unfolds, a tale of terror and self-discovery that will chill the very core of your being.

Our journey begins with Emily, a young woman plagued by an insatiable curiosity and a thirst for forbidden knowledge.

Drawn to the allure of the Looking Glass, an enigmatic mirror whispered to possess the power to pierce the veil between worlds, she finds herself standing before its ancient, reflective surface.

As Emily gazes into the mirror, a sense of unease washes over her.

The distorted reflection staring back at her seems to mock her very existence.

But the allure of the unknown beckons her forward, driving her to reach out and touch the cold, smooth surface of the Looking Glass.

In that instant, reality shatters like shards of glass, and Emily is thrust into a realm beyond comprehension.

The familiar world she once knew disintegrates into a twisted nightmare a labyrinth of distorted perspectives and maddening illusions.

Time bends and contorts, leaving her untethered in a realm where the laws of physics hold no sway.

Emily's journey through the Looking Glass becomes a descent into the darkest recesses of her own psyche. Each step forward reveals a fragment of her past, a haunting memory that claws its way to the sur-face.

The mirrors she encounters along the way are not mere reflections but gateways to forgotten moments, both beautiful and sinister, that have shaped her existence.

As she navigates the labyrinthine corridors, Emily encounters grotesque entities that seem to embody her deepest fears and regrets.

They lurk in the shadows, their eyes gleaming with a malevolence that pierces her soul.

They torment her with visions of her darkest secrets, forcing her to confront the choices she has made and the consequences they have borne.

The air is thick with whispers, a symphony of madness that echoes through the twisted corridors. Emily's own thoughts become tangled with the voices of the tormented souls who have ventured into the Looking Glass before her.

Their anguished cries mingle with her own, amplifying the sense of dread that permeates the air.

Each mirror becomes a portal to a different reality, a window into worlds that defy logic and reason.

Some reflect scenes of unimaginable horror, while others offer glimpses of ethereal beauty.

But behind every reflection lies a deeper truth an aspect of Emily's own self that she must confront if she is to find her way back to reality.

The Looking Glass revels in Emily's torment, its malevolent presence growing stronger with each passing moment.

It feeds off her fear, manipulating the mirrors to distort her perception and trap her in a never-ending cycle of self-reflection.

The line between nightmare and reality blurs, and Emily questions her own sanity.

Haunted by the malevolent forces that lurk within the Looking Glass, Emily musters every ounce of strength and resilience she possesses.

She delves deeper into the twisted labyrinth, determined to break free from its suffocating grasp.

Each step forward is a battle against the darkness threatening to consume her, a fight to reclaim her sanity and find a way back to the world she once knew.

But the Looking Glass is not so easily defeated. It watches and waits, its malevolence growing as Emily's resolve strengthens. It conjures illusions, distorting her perception and manipulating her deepest fears to immobilize her.

The mirrors multiply, creating a maddening maze of infinite reflections that confound her senses. In the depths of the Looking Glass, Emily encounters the embodiment of her own darkness a doppelganger that mirrors her form but possesses a malevolence beyond comprehension.

It taunts her, whispering cruel truths and luring her deeper into its clutches.

The battle for her soul intensifies, and Emily must confront the darkest aspects of her own nature if she is to emerge victorious. With every ounce of strength and determination, Emily confronts her doppelganger in a climactic showdown.

The two mirror images clash, their struggle a symphony of desperation and raw emotion.

The air crackles with energy as their powers collide, threatening to tear apart the very fabric of the twisted realm they inhabit.

In a final act of defiance, Emily shatters the mirror that holds her captive, breaking the hold of the Looking Glass on her mind and soul.

The realm of twisted nightmares crumbles around her, its malevolent power dissipated.

She emerges from the shattered fragments, battered, and scarred but triumphant.

In the aftermath of her harrowing journey through the Looking Glass, Emily's life is forever changed.

The experiences within the twisted realm have left an indelible mark on her psyche, haunting her dreams, and lingering in the corners of her waking thoughts.

She finds solace in therapy, seeking to unravel the tangled threads of her mind and make sense of the horrors she has witnessed.

But as Emily delves deeper into her therapy sessions, she begins to question the nature of her own reality.

Strange occurrences plague her daily life objects moving on their own, whispers echoing in empty rooms, and glimpses of distorted figures out of the corner of her eye.

The boundaries between the world of the Looking Glass and her own reality blur, leaving her uncertain of what is real and what is a product of her fractured mind.

Dr. Roberts, Emily's therapist, becomes increasingly intrigued by her case.

He delves into the lore surrounding the Looking Glass, searching for answers to the inexplicable events that have plagued Emily. His research leads him down a rabbit hole of ancient myths and forgotten legends, uncovering a web of dark secrets that stretch back centuries.

Meanwhile, Emily's nightmares intensify, the line between dream and reality growing ever thinner. She becomes obsessed with the notion that the Looking Glass is not just a figment of her imagination, but a doorway to something far more sinister.

She embarks on a quest to find others who have encountered the Looking Glass, hoping to find validation for her experiences and perhaps a way to bring an end to the horrors that haunt her.

In her search, Emily crosses paths with a mysterious group known as the Esoteric Society. Comprised of individuals who have themselves traversed the twisted realm of the Looking Glass, they offer her both solace and guidance.

Together, they unravel the enigmatic symbols and cryptic texts associated with the Looking Glass, piecing together the fragments of a long forgotten prophecy.

The prophecy speaks of an ancient entity, a malevolent force that seeks to break free from its prison within the Looking Glass and wreak havoc upon the world.

As Emily and the Esoteric Society delve deeper into the prophecy, they uncover a ritual a desperate gambit to seal the entity away once and for all.

With time running out, Emily and her newfound allies prepare to perform the ritual. They gather at the very spot where Emily first encountered the Looking Glass, a place where the boundaries between worlds are thinnest.

As the moon reaches its zenith, they begin the ceremony, channelling their collective energy and invoking ancient incantations.

But as the ritual progresses, the malevolent force within the Looking Glass fights back with a fury unmatched. Shadows dance and writhe, threatening to engulf them all.

Emily's own doppelganger, now infused with the essence of the ancient entity, emerges from the twisted depths of the mirror to thwart their efforts.

A battle ensues, a battle of wills, of darkness against light.

Emily and her allies fight with every ounce of strength, their determination fuelled by the horrors they have endured. The air crackles with magic and desperation, the outcome hanging in the balance.

In a climactic moment of sacrifice and bravery, Emily hurls herself into the depths of the Looking Glass, confronting her doppelganger head-on.

With a surge of inner strength, she merges with her dark reflection, absorbing the entity's power and imprisoning it within herself.

As Emily emerges from the Looking Glass, she carries the weight of the ancient entity within her, forever changed by its malevolence.

She becomes a guardian, a reluctant vessel of darkness, tasked with keeping the ancient force contained.

In the aftermath of the battle, Dr. Roberts reflects on the enigmatic nature of the Looking Glass and the mysteries that still linger.

He continues his research, seeking to understand the origins of the ancient entity and the true nature of the realm beyond the mirror.

And so, the tale of the Prologue to Looking Glass reaches its unsettling conclusion, leaving us with lingering questions and a sense of unease.

It serves as a chilling reminder that the boundaries of reality are fragile, and that even the most innocuous objects can hold unspeakable secrets.

The Looking Glass, once seen as a mere curiosity, becomes a symbol of the darkness that resides within us all, waiting to be unleashed.

The Nightingale

Once upon a time, in a world shrouded in darkness and despair, there existed a haunting tale known as The Nightingale.

It whispered through the ages, passed down from generation to generation, a chilling reminder of the perils that lay hidden in the shadows.

This is the extended and expanded retelling of that horrifying tale.

Deep in the heart of the cursed forest, where the moon's feeble light struggled to penetrate the thick canopy, lived Isabella a young woman burdened by a tragic past.

Haunted by the memories of loss and sorrow, she found solace in the melancholic songs of the nightingales that echoed through the trees.

Their haunting melodies were a bittersweet respite from the darkness that surrounded her.

But one fateful night, as Isabella wandered deeper into the forbidden depths of the forest, she stumbled upon a forgotten grove, bathed in an eerie luminescence.

The nightingales' songs grew louder, more alluring, beckoning her further into their enchanting embrace.

With each step, the air grew heavier, suffused with an ominous energy.

The trees twisted and contorted, their branches resembling gnarled fingers reaching out to ensnare the unwary traveller.

The once vibrant flora withered, their petals blackened and wilted, mirroring the decay that infested the cursed forest.

Isabella's heart pounded in her chest as she approached the source of the haunting melodies.

There, perched on a withered branch, sat a nightingale unlike any she had ever seen. Its feathers shimmered with an otherworldly glow, its eyes glinting with an intelligence that transcended the natural world.

This was no ordinary bird it was a creature of the night, its very essence intertwined with the dark forces that governed the forest.

Enthralled by its ethereal beauty, Isabella approached the nightingale, her hand outstretched.

As her fingertips brushed against its feathers, a surge of power coursed through her veins, intertwining their fates.

The nightingale's song intensified, its haunting melody weaving its way into her soul, whispering promises of unimaginable power and forbidden knowledge.

But with every gift, there comes a price.

Unbeknownst to Isabella, the nightingale was cursed a creature bound to the darkness, its captivating song a siren's call that lured unsuspecting souls to their doom.

The nightingale's true nature was that of a malevolent trickster, a harbinger of chaos and despair. As the nightingale's influence grew, so did the forest's transformation.

The once tranquil haven turned into a twisted realm of nightmares.

The trees groaned with the weight of their torment, their gnarled branches contorting into grotesque shapes that resembled tortured souls.

The ground beneath Isabella's feet quivered with unease, as if the very earth itself rebelled against the curse that gripped it.

It wasn't long before Isabella realized the extent of her mistake. The power she had acquired came at a steep cost her sanity and the lives of those she held dear.

The nightingale's demands grew insatiable, its songs haunting her every waking moment.

Sleep became a distant memory, replaced by feverish visions and haunting nightmares that seemed to merge with reality.

As Isabella's mind unravelled, the forest mirrored her descent into madness.

Dark, ethereal beings emerged from the shadows, their twisted forms contorting and writhing in a macabre dance.

They whispered dark secrets and revelled in her torment, their wicked laughter echoing through the cursed woods.

In her darkest hour, Isabella knew she had to break free from the nightingale's grip.

With a newfound determination, she embarked on a perilous journey a quest to find the ancient tome that held the key to undoing the curse.

The journey was fraught with peril, as the forest itself seemed to conspire against her, sending grotesque creatures to impede her progress.

The nightmarish creatures she encountered grew more grotesque and violent.

Their gnarled limbs and distorted features dripped with blood and oozed with foul substances.

They lunged at Isabella with ferocious intent, their claws tearing through the air, hungry for her flesh. Their distorted screams filled the forest, merging into a cacophony of pure madness.

But Isabella pressed on, her will unyielding. She faced nightmarish trials and battles against the forces of darkness, drawing upon a hidden strength buried deep within her soul.

The nightingale's influence waned with each step, its power weakening as Isabella grew closer to her goal. Isabella's own fears and regrets materialized before her eyes, taking on physical forms that haunted her every step.

She was pursued by the Spectres of her past, their ghostly presence a constant reminder of her own guilt and the darkness that resided within her soul.

The forest itself seemed to feed off her fear, twisting and contorting to amplify her anguish.

The nightingale, no longer a creature of beauty, perched on a grotesque throne made of the bones of its victims.

Its once melodious song had transformed into a haunting dirge, a symphony of despair that seeped into Isabella's very core.

Its eyes glowed with an unnatural light, filled with the malevolent glee of a sadistic tormentor.

Finally, after what felt like an eternity, Isabella stood before the ancient tome a weathered, leather-bound book whispered to contain the knowledge needed to break the curse.

With trembling hands, she pried it open, its pages filled with cryptic symbols and arcane incantations.

Driven by desperation, Isabella poured over the ancient text, deciphering its secrets, and piecing together the ritual that could sever the bond between her and the nightingale.

She assembled the necessary ingredients, her heart pounding with a mix of fear and hope.

As the moon reached its zenith, casting a pale glow over the forest, Isabella performed the ritual a complex dance of incantations and blood offerings.

The nightingale's song filled the air, its melody a cacophony of triumph and defiance.

But Isabella's resolve remained unshaken. With a final surge of energy, she completed the ritual, severing the bond that had ensnared her soul. The forest trembled, its torment dissipating like a fleeting nightmare.

The nightingale's form flickered, its luminous feathers dulling to a lifeless Gray.

With a mournful cry, it vanished into the night Isabella stood alone in the now peaceful forest, her body battered and scarred, but her spirit unyielding.

She had faced the darkest corners of her soul and emerged triumphant, breaking the curse that had plagued the nightingale and the forest for centuries.

Exhausted and scarred by her harrowing journey, Isabella emerged from the cursed depths, forever changed.

The nightingale's curse had left its mark a constant reminder of the horrors she had faced and the darkness she had conquered.

Isabella stood alone in the now peaceful forest, her body battered and scarred, but her spirit unyielding.

She had faced the darkest corners of her soul and emerged triumphant, breaking the curse that had plagued the nightingale and the forest for centuries.

Yet, as she turned to leave, a faint whisper reached her ears a haunting melody that carried on the wind. It was the nightingale's final song, a melancholic reminder of the horrors that had unfolded.

Isabella couldn't help but shudder, knowing that the echoes of that cursed melody would forever linger in the depths of her mind.

As she ventured back into the world beyond the forest, Isabella carried with her the knowledge of the nightingale's true nature a cautionary tale of the dangers that lie hidden in enchanting melodies and promises of power.

She became a guardian of the woods, warning others of the cursed nightingale's allure and the treacherous path it led.

And so, the tale of The Nightingale stands as a chilling testament to the corrupting power of desire and the resilience of the human spirit.

It serves as a haunting reminder that even the most beautiful melodies can mask a malevolent intent and that true strength lies in confronting and overcoming one's darkest fears.

In the annals of adult horror tales, The Nightingale remains etched as a chilling reminder of the price one may pay for succumbing to forbidden allure and the enduring power of redemption.

"IN THE FACE OF UNIMAGINABLE TRIALS, THE HUMAN SPIRIT ENDURES. WE ARE SURVIVORS, WARRIORS WHO HAVE FACED THE DEPTHS OF DARKNESS AND EMERGED STRONGER THAN BEFORE. OUR SCARS TELL STORIES OF RESILIENCE AND OUR HEARTS SHINE WITH THE LIGHT OF RESILIENCE. WITH EVERY STEP
FORWARD, WE REDEFINE OUR OWN NARRATIVE, FORGING A PATH OF HEALING AND REMINDING THE WORLD THAT SURVIVAL IS NOT JUST A POSSIBILITY,
BUT A TESTAMENT TO THE STRENGTH WITHIN US ALL."

QUOTE BY ANGELESS WATKINS-GALLAR

The Dark Secrets of Fairy Tales

Act 3

THE SPINDLE, THE SHUTTLE, AND THE NEEDLE

In a forgotten village shrouded in a perpetual twilight, a chilling tale unfolded. The spindle, the shuttle, and the needle, once symbols of domesticity and craftsmanship, became harbingers of terror and des-pair. A curse had befallen the land, transforming the innocuous tools into instruments of malevolence.

The curse emanated from an ancient tapestry, said to possess a dark and mysterious power. Within its intricate patterns lay the key to an otherworldly realm a realm where nightmares were made flesh and dreams turned into unspeakable horrors.

Legends whispered that whoever dared to weave upon the cursed tapestry would unleash a force that would forever alter their fate.

In the heart of the village lived a young woman named Eliza, renowned for her weaving skills and gentle nature. Drawn to the allure of the forbidden, she succumbed to temptation and ventured into the forbidden chamber where the tapestry resided.

Ignoring the warnings of the elders, Eliza took up the spindle, the shuttle, and the needle, their once innocent forms now twisted and sinister.

In the depths of the cursed village, the horrors escalated as the curse tightened its grip on the unsuspecting inhabitants. The nightmares that plagued their slumber spilled into their waking hours, blurring the line between reality and the macabre.

The once tranquil streets became haunted by spectral figures, their ethereal forms floating amidst the shadows. Their hollow eyes fixated on the terrified villagers, filling them with a sense of dread that seeped into their bones.

The air itself carried an oppressive weight, suffocating their every breath with an aura of malevolence.

As Eliza began to weave upon the cursed tapestry, the very fabric of reality began to unravel. Shadows crept along the walls, whispering secrets too terrible to comprehend. The village, once a place of serenity, transformed into a nightmare realm where nightmares roamed freely.

With each stitch, Eliza unwittingly bound herself to the malevolent forces lurking within the tapestry. The spindle spun threads of darkness, entwining her mind and soul. The shuttle wove a web of despair, ensnaring her in its cold embrace.

And the needle pierced her heart, injecting a poison that consumed her from within.

As Eliza succumbed further to the curse, her transformation into a vessel of darkness intensified. Her once soothing voice now echoed with a chilling resonance, whispering ancient incantations that summoned forth abominations from the depths of the tapestry.

Grotesque creatures, stitched together from nightmares, roamed the village, preying upon the vulnerable.

The villagers, driven to the brink of madness, began to lose their grip on reality. They were tormented by vivid hallucinations, forced to confront their deepest fears and regrets.

Shadows danced along the walls, contorting into twisted shapes that taunted their sanity. The boundary between life and death grew thin, as the spirits of the cursed whispered eerie laments in their ears.

In the heart of the cursed tapestry's chamber, where the veil between worlds was thinnest, a ritual of unspeakable horror took place. Eliza, under the influence of the spindle, the shuttle, and the needle, orchestrated a dark ceremony that merged the physical realm with the nightmares woven into the fabric.

The skies darkened, engulfing the village in an eternal night. The moon itself twisted into a sickly hue, casting an eerie glow upon the desolation. Unholy cries pierced the air as the boundaries between dimensions shattered, allowing eldritch beings to spill forth into the mortal realm.

Their forms defied comprehension, their mere presence inducing terror beyond imagination.

The villagers, desperate to break free from the clutches of the curse, embarked on a perilous journey through the twisted land-scape that now surrounded them.

They traversed through nightmarish forests, where trees bled black ichor and whispered malicious secrets. They encountered grotesque creatures that hungered for their souls, their forms twisted and contorted in unimaginable ways.

The villagers, once bound by a sense of community and unity, now turned on each other in a frenzy of paranoia and fear. As the curse tightened its grip, the once vibrant colours of the village faded into shades of Gray.

The very fabric of reality seemed to warp and distort, mirroring the twisted nature of the curse itself. Strange occurrences plagued the villagers at every turn, objects moved of their own accord, whispers echoed through empty corridors, and ghostly apparitions materialized in the corners of their vision.

The curse fed on the desperation and despair of the villagers, manipulating their deepest desires and fears. It whispered sinister promises of power and beauty, tempting them to surrender their souls in exchange for a brief respite from their suffering.

Those who succumbed to the allure found themselves trapped in an eternal nightmare, their bodies twisted and their minds forever tormented.

In the heart of the village stood a towering mansion, shrouded in darkness and mystery. It was rumoured to be the source of the curse, a place where the spindle, the shuttle, and the needle resided, weaving their wicked spells into the tapestry of the villagers' lives.

The mansion stood as a foreboding symbol, drawing the brave and the foolhardy into its web of malevolence.

Few dared to enter the mansion, but those who did were confronted with a labyrinth of twisted corridors and shadowy chambers.

Each room held its own macabre secret from grotesque experiments conducted by an ancient sorcerer to rooms filled with haunting echoes of past tragedies. The walls seemed to pulse with a malevolent energy, and the air was thick with a suffocating sense of dread. As the villagers ventured deeper into the mansion, they discovered a hidden chamber where the cursed artifacts lay dormant.

The spindle, once an innocuous tool of creation, now radiated an aura of darkness that sent shivers down their spines. The shuttle, once a symbol of creativity and skill, dripped with the blood of the innocent. And the needle, once a humble instrument of stitching, now possessed an insidious power to pierce the very fabric of reality.

In their quest to break the curse, the villagers faced unimaginable horrors. They battled grotesque creatures spawned from their own twisted nightmares, their bodies contorted and deformed into monstrous visages.

The curse amplified their darkest desires and fears, turning them against each other in a desperate struggle for survival. As the final confrontation loomed, the villagers found themselves face to face with the embodiment of the curse itself.

A malevolent entity, born from the amalgamation of their collective pain and suffering, stood as the harbinger of their doom. Its eyes glowed with an unholy light, and its voice echoed with the anguish of a thousand souls.

The battle that ensued was a symphony of bloodshed and horror. The villagers fought with every ounce of their strength, wielding the power of their collective will to confront the curse head-on.

Their bodies bore the scars of their ordeal, their minds teetering on the edge of madness, but they pressed on fuelled by a newfound determination to break free from the curse's grip.

In a climactic struggle, the cursed artifacts were destroyed, their power shattered into oblivion. The curse unravelled, dissipating like a dark mist, and the mansion itself crumbled into ruins.

The villagers, battered and broken but triumphant, emerged from the ordeal forever changed.

The spindle, the shuttle, and the needle were reduced to fragments of their former selves, mere relics of a dark past.

The curse, while vanquished, left a lasting mark on the villagers. They carried the weight of their experiences, forever haunted by the horrors they had witnessed and the choices they had made.

In the aftermath, the villagers found solace in rebuilding their lives and restoring their shattered community. They vowed to never forget the lessons learned from the curse and to cherish the fragile beauty of their existence.

The spindle, the shuttle, and the needle became symbols of resilience and the enduring power of the human spirit to overcome even the darkest of forces.

They carried the weight of their experiences, forever haunted by the horrors they had witnessed and the choices they had made. In the aftermath, the villagers found solace in rebuilding their lives and restoring their shattered community.

They vowed to never forget the lessons learned from the curse and to cherish the fragile beauty of their existence. The spindle, the shuttle, and the needle became symbols of resilience and the enduring power of the human spirit to overcome even the darkest of forces.

And so, dear reader, let this tale of the spindle, the shuttle, and the needle serve as a chilling reminder of the price one can pay for their insatiable curiosity. It warns of the dangers that lie within the forbid-den realms of magic and the nightmares that can be unleashed upon the world.

May it serve as a haunting testament to the fragility of the human spirit and the eternal struggle against the darkness that surround

The duration of life

Deep within the mist-shrouded forest, where time danced to an eerie rhythm and the whisper of leaves carried the secrets of the ages, there existed a peculiar village known as Eldervale.

The village was cursed with a haunting tale that echoed through the hearts and minds of its inhabitants the tale of

"The Duration of Life."

Legend spoke of a dark enchantment that had befallen Eldervale, where the duration of life was no longer bound by the natural order. In this twisted realm, the aging process was accelerated, and time became a relentless tormentor, stealing away the vitality and beauty of its inhabitants with each passing day.

At the heart of the village stood an ancient clocktower, its towering presence casting a sinister shadow over Eldervale. Within its ornate structure lay the secret to the curse the Timekeeper's Clock.

Legend spoke of a mysterious figure, a malevolent being known as the Timekeeper, who held dominion over the flow of time itself, wielding it as a weapon to punish and torment the villagers.

The villagers, their once youthful faces now etched with the weariness of premature age, gathered in hushed whispers to discuss the forbidden rituals and desperate bargains that promised a chance at eternal youth.

Whispers of sacrifices made in darkened corners, of blood spilled upon ancient soils, and of rituals that danced precariously on the edge of madness, circulated among the desperate souls who craved respite from the relentless march of time.

One fateful night, a young woman named Evelyn found herself drawn into the web of the Timekeeper's curse.

Fearful for her own fleeting existence and consumed by the sorrowful plight of her fellow villagers, she delved deep into the forbidden knowledge hidden within the village's archives.

Guided by half-erased manuscripts, cryptic symbols, and the remnants of forgotten incantations, she uncovered the ancient rituals that promised an escape from the ravages of time.

Driven by desperation, Evelyn embarked on a treacherous journey to confront the Timekeeper, determined to break the curse that had shackled Eldervale in its cruel grip for far too long.

She traversed the treacherous forest, its gnarled trees whispering eerie secrets and its dense undergrowth hiding the remnants of those who had ventured before her.

Through moonlit glades and winding paths, Evelyn followed the echoes of a haunting melody that seemed to emanate from the heart of the clocktower. The melody grew louder with each step, its haunting notes tinged with both sorrow and a twisted sense of power.

As Evelyn stepped through the imposing doors of the clocktower, the air thickened with an oppressive weight. Shadows danced and swirled, revealing glimpses of grotesque manifestations of time's corruption.

Monstrous creatures, once innocent villagers now twisted and malformed, lurched forward, their eyes vacant yet filled with an insatiable hunger for eternal life.

Evelyn's heart raced, her grip tightening on the dagger she carried, for she knew that her every step brought her closer to her own confrontation with the Timekeeper.

Finally, she reached the chamber where the Timekeeper awaited, an entity draped in shadows, its face obscured by an ancient clockwork mask.

The Timekeeper's voice echoed with a chilling melody, a haunting reminder of the fleeting nature of existence.

It spoke of the fragility of time, of the balance between life and death, and of the consequences that awaited those who dared to defy its dominion.

The Time-keeper offered Evelyn a choice to embrace the curse, to become one of its eternal guardians, or to face the dire consequences of her defiance.

The weight of the villagers' hopes rested upon her shoulders as she stood before the malevolent entity, her heart torn between self-preservation and the greater good.

In a moment of clarity and courage, Evelyn renounced the allure of eternal youth and defied the Timekeeper's wicked proposition. She wielded her dagger with unwavering determination, striking at the very heart of the cursed clockwork mask that had veiled the Timekeeper's true form.

As the mask shattered into a thousand shards, the Timekeeper's true visage was revealed a grotesque amalgamation of withered flesh and coiling shadows. It let out a bone chilling scream, its existence unravelling like the ticking of a broken clock.

As Evelyn emerged from the depths of the abyss, the village of Eldervale basked in the newfound light of freedom. The curse that had plagued them for generations was finally broken, and the villagers celebrated with a mixture of relief and joy.

But even as they rejoiced, a lingering unease settled in the air. Evelyn, hailed as a saviour by the villagers, bore the weight of her harrowing journey.

The horrors she had witnessed in her battle against the Embodiment of Time haunted her dreams, the echoes of its malevolent laughter reverberating in her mind.

She had stared into the abyss and emerged forever changed.

The once vibrant village now wore the scars of the curse. The effects of accelerated aging had left its mark, even in the moments of their restored youth.

Lines etched deeper on their faces, shadows of the time stolen from them. Laughter held a tinge of sadness, and the villagers couldn't shake the feeling of impending doom.

Evelyn, plagued by guilt and a deep sense of responsibility, sought solace in the ancient texts and forbidden knowledge that had led her to the Timekeeper's chamber. She delved into the dark arts, determined to uncover the secrets that lay hidden beneath the surface of the curse.

In her relentless pursuit of understanding, Evelyn stumbled upon a dark prophecy buried within the depths of an ancient tomb. It spoke of a hidden price, a sacrifice that had been made to unleash the curse upon the village.

The curse had been an act of revenge, a twisted punishment inflicted upon the ancestors of Eldervale.

The prophecy warned of a reckoning a time when the curse would seek retribution, demanding the life force of those who had dared to defy its grip. The Embodiment of Time had been but a harbinger, a vessel through which the curse exacted its vengeance.

As Evelyn shared her findings with the villagers, a collective unease settled over Eldervale. Whispers of the prophecy spread like wildfire, and a sense of impending doom hung heavy in the air.

The curse had been broken, but the price had yet to be paid. Days turned into nights, and the villagers lived on borrowed time, each moment tinged with a haunting sense of inevitability.

Shadows danced in the corners of their vision, and the village seemed to grow colder as an unseen presence drew closer. Then, one fateful night, as the moon reached its zenith, a foreboding silence fell over Eldervale.

The village lay shrouded in darkness, the absence of sound a haunting reminder of the impending doom. The villagers huddled in their homes, trembling with fear, as they awaited the arrival of the curse's final judgment.

And as the midnight hour struck, the curse revealed its true nature. Shadows coalesced into tangible forms, crawling along the ground like living tendrils.

Whispers of the ancient curse echoed through the village, chilling the very souls of those who heard them.

One by one, the villagers succumbed to the curse's demands. Time, once stolen, was now reclaimed with a vengeance. The effects of accelerated aging returned, but this time, there was no reprieve.

The villagers aged rapidly, their bodies withering away as the curse drained their life force. Evelyn, burdened by guilt and a determination to right the wrongs, stepped forward.

She stood in the centre of the village square, her voice strong and unwavering, as she addressed the curse itself. She spoke of the injustices suffered, the sacrifices made, and the power of redemption.

In a desperate act of defiance, Evelyn offered herself as the final sacrifice a willing vessel for the curse's retribution. She knew the curse had to be appeased, but she also believed in the power of selflessness and sacrifice. With every fibre of her being, she hoped to break the cycle of vengeance and bring an end to the torment that had plagued Eldervale for generations.

As Evelyn stood before the curse, her body aged before the villagers' eyes. Wrinkles etched deeper, hair turned Gray, and her once vibrant spirit flickered in the face of imminent demise.

But within that sacrifice, she found a glimmer of hope a chance for redemption and the possibility of breaking the curse's hold on Eldervale.

In her final moments, Evelyn whispered words of forgiveness, releasing the curse from its cycle of vengeance.

And as her life force dissipated into the night, a blinding light engulfed the village, banishing the curse and restoring peace to Eldervale.

Eldervale, forever changed by the horrors it had endured, emerged from the shadows with a newfound appreciation for the fragility and beauty of life.

The scars remained, a constant reminder of the dark-ness they had faced, but they carried within them a resilience and strength that would guide them through the darkest of times.

And so, dear reader, let the tale of "The Duration of Life" serve as a chilling reminder of the consequences of revenge and the power of sacrifice.

May it stand as a testament to the indomitable spirit of humanity, even in the face of the most harrowing horrors, and a warning of the lasting impact that our actions can have on the fabric of existence.

The ugly ducking

Once upon a time, in a forgotten corner of a grim and unforgiving world, there existed a young woman named Adelaide. She was born into a society obsessed with beauty and perfection, where appearances were valued above all else.

But Adelaide, with her unconventional features and mismatched eyes, stood out like a sore thumb in this sea of uniformity.

From the moment she entered the world, Adelaide was met with ridicule and scorn. The villagers, blinded by their narrow definition of beauty, mocked her relentlessly.

They called her "ugly" and "hideous," their words seeping into her vulnerable mind like poison.

Adelaide grew up haunted by their hurtful words, carrying the weight of their judgment upon her fragile shoulders. She began to internalize their cruelty, believing herself to be truly repulsive.

The seeds of self-doubt and insecurity were sown deep within her, taking root, and growing into a tangled mess of psychological torment.

As she gazed into the mirror, Adelaide saw a distorted reflection staring back at her a reflection warped by the villagers' hateful words.

Their voices echoed in her mind, whispering that she was unworthy of love, that her existence was an affront to beauty itself.

Isolation became her refuge. She withdrew from society, seeking solace in the solitude of the forest that surrounded her isolated home.

The trees became her only confidants, their silent presence offering more comfort than the company of her fellow villagers ever could. In the depths of her isolation, Ade-laide forged a connection with the creatures that roamed the shadows.

The animals, with their innocent eyes and non-judgmental nature, provided a respite from the harsh realities of human cruelty. They became her only source of affection and acceptance.

One fateful day, while wandering through the forest, Adelaide stumbled upon a peculiar pond. Its tranquil waters seemed to hold a glimmer of understanding, a reflection of her inner turmoil.

Overwhelmed by despair, she cried out, pouring her heartache into the abyss.

To her surprise, the heavens answered. A haunting melody floated through the air, and a figure emerged from the depths of the pond. It was a sinister being, known as the Enchantress of Transformation, a master of dark magic.

The Enchantress offered Adelaide a chance to change her fate, to escape the torment that had plagued her existence.

Desperate for an escape from the psychological prison she had been trapped in, Adelaide accepted the Enchantress's offer without hesitation. The Enchantress cast a powerful spell, transforming Adelaide into a beautiful woman with flawless features—a stark contrast to the ugliness she had believed herself to possess.

Adelaide's external transformation brought her temporary relief.

The villagers, now captivated by her beauty, treated her with newfound respect and admiration.

But the scars of their hurtful words remained etched within her psyche, festering like an infected wound.

As Adelaide basked in the fleeting adulation, the villagers' shallow affection felt hollow and empty. She became acutely aware of their superficiality, their shallow nature.

Each compliment bestowed upon her felt like a thinly veiled mockery, a reminder of the cruelty that lay beneath their polite facades.

Inwardly, Adelaide struggled with a distorted self-image. The internalized voices of the villagers continued to haunt her, poisoning her perception of herself.

She saw herself as a fraud, an imposter hiding behind a mask of beauty, forever burdened by the ugliness that she believed lurked within. Adelaide's hunger for validation grew insatiable, her psychological torment driving her to desperate measures.

She devoured the compliments and admiration, seeking to fill the void left by the villagers' hurtful words. But no amount of praise could silence the voices within, for they had become ingrained in the very fabric of her being.

With each passing day, Adelaide's appearance began to decay, her true nature seeping through the cracks. The façade of beauty crumbled, revealing the twisted remnants of the insecure young woman she had always been.

Her once flawless skin became marred with dark, grotesque patches a physical manifestation of the psychological scars she carried. Haunted by her curse and tormented by her own reflection, Adelaide retreated into the darkness once more.

The forest, now a twisted labyrinth of her own making, became her prison. She roamed the shadows, a pitiful creature driven by a bottomless hunger and an unquenchable thirst for beauty that would never be satisfied. Word of Adelaide's curse spread like wildfire through the land.

Fear and fascination grew, as people whispered tales of the ravenous beauty who devoured the souls of those she encountered.

The once-idyllic village lived in perpetual dread, their hearts burdened by the shadow of the Ugly Duckling turned monstrous. One brave soul, a compassionate traveller named Edward, dared to venture into the heart of the forest, determined to confront the creature that haunted their nightmares.

With a heart filled with empathy and a soul un-touched by vanity, he saw past the outward appearance and recognized the pain that consumed Adelaide.

As Edward approached Adelaide, her hunger raged within her, urging her to consume yet another innocent soul.

But Edward, driven by compassion, offered her something she had never experienced genuine kindness and acceptance. He saw beyond her monstrous façade, reaching out to the broken soul within.

In that moment, something within Adelaide stirred a flicker of humanity that had long been dormant. Touched by Edward's compassion, she surrendered herself to his mercy, longing for redemption from the curse that had consumed her.

Edward, refusing to succumb to fear or hatred, devised a plan to break the curse that had imprisoned Adelaide.

Together, they embarked on a perilous journey, facing trials and temptations that sought to test their resolve.

They confronted the Enchantress of Transformation, the source of Adelaide's curse, and demanded that she release them from their torment.

The Enchantress, intrigued by their unwavering love and determination, offered them a choice. They could either continue living in the cursed existence they had known, forever hungering for beauty, or they could embrace their true selves, accepting their flaws and finding solace in genuine love.

Adelaide and Edward chose the latter, rejecting the false allure of beauty in favour of a life guided by compassion and authenticity.

The Enchantress, impressed by their choice, lifted the curse that had plagued them, releasing them from their prison of eternal hunger. As the curse was broken, Adelaide's appearance transformed once again.

But this time, it was not into a superficial beauty that mesmerized the eyes, but into a reflection of her true self a woman scarred by her past but resilient and unyielding in her journey towards self-acceptance.

Adelaide and Edward returned to the village, not as objects of fear and fascination, but as symbols of hope and redemption. They shared their story, shedding light on the impact of hurtful words and the long-lasting scars they can leave behind.

The village, touched by their transformation, embraced a new era of empathy, where the power of kindness and acceptance was celebrated.

And so, the tale of the Ugly Duckling took on a dark twist, delving into the depths of vanity, hunger, and the transformative power of self-acceptance. It served as a haunting reminder that true beauty lies not in appearances alone, but in the depths of one's character and the capacity to love without conditions.

In the annals of adult horror tales, the story of Adelaide, the Ugly Duckling, became a testament to the dangers of societal expectations and the liberation found in embracing one's true self.

It warned of the consequences of sacrificing authenticity for the pursuit of superficial beauty and offered a glimmer of hope that redemption is possible, even for those haunted by their own demons.

THUMBELINA

In a forgotten corner of a shadowy forest, where the trees whispered ancient secrets and the moon rarely cast its light, there lived a lonely woman named Helena. She yearned for the joy of motherhood with an intensity that consumed her every waking moment.

The ache in her heart grew with each passing day, casting a shadow over her existence.

As Helena watched other families frolic in the village, her yearning intensified. She longed to hold a child of her own, to experience the purest form of love and connection.

But fate had dealt her a cruel hand, denying her the gift of motherhood. Helena's desperation caught the attention of a malevolent enchantress who revelled in toying with the emotions of mortals.

The enchantress, known for her powers of perception and manipulation, sensed Helena's vulnerability and decided to exploit it for her own dark amusement. Appearing before Helena in a veil of ethereal mist, the enchantress offered her a deal that seemed too good to be true.

"I can grant your deepest wish," she whispered, her voice a seductive melody.

"But know that every gift comes with a price."

Eager to fill the void within her, Helena agreed without hesitation. The enchantress handed her a small vial containing a mysterious elixir.

"Drink this potion," the enchantress whispered, "and your wish shall be granted."

Helena, blinded by her longing, ignored the warning, and accepted the enchantress's offer without hesitation. Unbeknownst to her, the enchantress's powers of perception allowed her to see into them deepest recesses of Helena's soul, uncovering her innermost desires and vulnerabilities.

Using her powers, the enchantress weaved a spell that twisted Helena's perception of reality.

She manipulated her thoughts, filling her mind with illusions of a perfect life as a mother, while concealing the darkness that lurked beneath the surface.

Days turned into weeks, and Helena's belly swelled with the promise of new life. She revelled in the blissful delusion of impending motherhood, unaware of the enchantress's curse that had taken root within her unborn child.

But as the months passed, a darkness settled upon Helena's spirit. The elixir's effects twisted her perception, filling her mind with irrational fears and haunting visions. Nightmares plagued her sleep, foretelling of a dreadful fate that awaited her unborn child.

Helena's once-glowing anticipation turned into a gnawing anxiety that gnawed at her sanity. Doubt consumed her, whispering poisonous thoughts that her child would be monstrous, a creature that brought only suffering and despair.

As her due date approached, Helena's mind teetered on the brink of madness. The weight of her fears crushed her spirit, overshadowing the joy that should have accompanied the impending arrival of her child.

The moment of birth arrived, and Helena brought forth a child unlike any other. The infant emerged from her womb with translucent skin, eyes that mirrored the depths of her own torment, and a piercing cry that chilled the hearts of those who heard it.

Whispers spread through the village; tales of the cursed child born of Helena's desperate longing. Fear and superstition cast a shadow over the infant's life, branding her as an abomination.

When Thumbelina was born, the enchantress's curse revealed itself in her soul. It manifested as a dark stain that tainted her every thought and action.

The curse influenced her perception of the world, distorting her view of reality and filling her heart with a deep-rooted despair.

From a young age, Thumbelina felt the weight of the curse upon her. She perceived the world through a distorted lens, where love and acceptance were elusive, replaced by feelings of isolation and self-loathing.

The enchantress's curse whispered venomous thoughts into her mind, convincing her that she was unworthy of happiness and destined to bring pain to those around her.

As Thumbelina grew older, her powers of perception heightened, allowing her to sense the true nature of those she encountered. She could see through their facades, their hidden intentions, and darkest secrets.

The curse twisted this ability, making her perceive everyone as a potential threat, turning her own heart cold and distant. Trapped in the clutches of the curse, Thumbelina's perception of herself became increasingly distorted.

She saw herself as a monster, a vessel of darkness that could only bring suffering to others. The curse fed on her insecurities, reinforcing her negative self-image, and pushing her further into the depths of despair. But deep within her tormented soul, a flicker of defiance ignited.

She yearned to break free from the enchantress's curse, to forge her own path and find redemption. With every ounce of strength, she could muster, she sought ways to counteract the curse's influence, clinging to the sliver of hope that remained.

Thumbelina 's journey was arduous and treacherous, as she navigated the labyrinth of her own mind, confronting her deepest fears and insecurities.

The enchantress's curse haunted her every step, testing her resolve and tempting her to succumb to the darkness.

Along the way, Thumbelina encountered kindred spirits who saw through the curse's veil and offered her their support and guidance.

They recognized her inner strength and helped her harness her powers of perception for good, to see beyond the surface and find the beauty and potential in herself and others.

Through their love and unwavering belief in her inherent goodness, she discovered the power of self-acceptance and forgiveness. She realized that her perception of herself had been distorted by the curse, and that she had the strength within her to break free from its hold.

With each step she took towards self-discovery, Thumbelina chipped away at the enchantress's curse, liberating herself from the chains that had bound her for so long.

She emerged from the shadows; her perception of the world forever altered.

No longer a victim of the curse, she became a beacon of light, using her powers to bring healing and empathy to those she encountered.

As Thumbelina 's influence spread, the enchantress grew furious at the loss of her prized pawn.

She launched one final assault, seeking to reclaim control over her own shattered soul. But now Thumbelina, armed with her newfound strength and the love and support of those she had touched, stood firm against the enchantress's onslaught.

In a climactic battle between light and darkness, Thumbelina confronted the enchantress, their powers clashing in a torrent of energy.

The enchantress's curse, once formidable, withered under Thumbelina 's resilience and determination. With a final surge of power, the curse was shattered, banishing the enchantress and reclaiming her freedom.

The village, once consumed by fear and superstition, witnessed Thumbelina 's transformation and redemption. They saw her for the beacon of hope she had become, a testament to the power of self-discovery and the strength to rise above the darkness that threatened to consume her.

And so, the tale of Thumbelina weaves a tapestry of horror, desire, and the enduring struggle for love and acceptance.

It serves as a haunting reminder that the deepest yearnings can both uplift and destroy, leaving scars upon the soul that can only be healed through compassion and self-forgiveness.

The Snow Queen

In a desolate village blanketed by eternal winter, the Snow Queen reigned with an icy grip. Her presence cast a shadow of fear and despair over the land, freezing the hearts of all who dared to oppose her.

Rumours whispered that she possessed supernatural powers, capable of freezing souls and turning the innocent into servants of darkness.

From a young age, the villagers were indoctrinated with stories of the Snow Queen's wrath. They were told that her icy touch could freeze their souls and that her piercing gaze could strip away their humanity.

These tales became deeply ingrained in their consciousness, fuelling their fear, and shaping their behaviour.

The Snow Queen's influence permeated every aspect of the villagers' lives. They lived in constant anticipation of her next move, tiptoeing through their existence, lest they provoke her wrath.

Their fear dictated their actions, causing them to shrink away from anything that might attract the Snow Queen's attention.

Children were raised to be silent and obedient, taught that curiosity and rebellion would invite the Snow Queen's icy grasp.

Their youthful innocence was replaced by a constant state of vigilance, as they tiptoed through their days, their laughter stifled by the weight of their fear.

The adults, too, succumbed to the Snow Queen's psychological hold. Their lives revolved around caution and conformity, their dreams and aspirations snuffed out by the chilling presence that dominated their thoughts.

They lived in a state of perpetual anxiety, their minds clouded by the constant dread of what the Snow Queen might do next.

The Snow Queen revelled in their fear, feeding off their collective despair. She delighted in their paranoia, whispering malicious thoughts into their minds and sowing seeds of doubt and self-doubt.

Her icy tendrils invaded their dreams, transforming them into haunting nightmares that left them sleepless and haunted.

Amidst the villagers' terror, there lived a young woman named Isabella, whose spirit refused to be extinguished by the Snow Queen's malevolence. Isabella, unlike the others, dared to question the narrative that had been forced upon them.

She yearned for freedom from the suffocating fear that had held the villagers captive for far too long.

Isabella's defiance did not go unnoticed by the Snow Queen. Intrigued by her audacity, the Snow Queen turned her attention to Isabella, determined to break her spirit and use her as an example to quell any thoughts of rebellion that might arise among the villagers.

As Isabella slept peacefully in her cottage, a bitter gust of wind blew open her window, allowing the Snow Queen's frosty breath to enter. Isabella's eyes snapped open, and her heart pounded with unease as she sensed a menacing presence in the room.

She could feel the cold seeping into her bones, paralyzing her with fear. A haunting voice echoed through the room,

"You are mine now, Isabella. Your beauty will serve a higher purpose, as you become an instrument of my icy reign."

Isabella's body trembled as the Snow Queen's words sank into her soul. As Isabella delved deeper into the psychological realm, her encounters with the Snow Queen became more intense.

The Snow Queen manipulated her fears, conjuring vivid nightmares that taunted Isabella's every step.

She found herself trapped in mazes of doubt and despair, where the walls whispered haunting truths and the floor threatened to crumble beneath her feet.

But Isabella refused to surrender to the Snow Queen's psychological torment. She called upon her inner strength, mustering the courage to face her fears head-on.

She challenged the illusions and questioned the authenticity of her own thoughts. Slowly, she began to unravel the web of deception the Snow Queen had spun around her.

From that night onward, Isabella's life became a living nightmare. The Snow Queen's enchantment twisted her perception, transforming her into a mere puppet under the Queen's command.

Her once-vibrant spirit withered, replaced by a cold detachment that mirrored the Snow Queen's own icy demeanour.

Isabella was forced to carry out the Queen's sinister bidding, spreading the eternal winter further into the hearts of the villagers. With each passing day, her beauty faded, replaced by a pale, ghostly visage that reflected the darkness that consumed her.

Her touch turned everything she encountered into ice, leaving a trail of desolation in her wake.

As the village plunged deeper into despair, hope flickered in the form of a young man named Markus.

He had heard tales of the Snow Queen's wicked reign and the fate that had befallen Isabella.

Driven by love and a desire to free her from the Queen's clutches, Markus embarked on a perilous journey to confront the Snow Queen and break her hold over Isabella.

Guided by a sage old woman who possessed ancient knowledge of the Snow Queen's powers, Markus traversed treacherous landscapes, braving bone-chilling blizzards and encountering malevolent creatures born of the Queen's dark magic.

He knew that his love for Isabella would be tested, but he pressed on with unwavering determination.

Finally, Markus stood before the Snow Queen's frozen palace, a towering structure that radiated an aura of pure evil.

He confronted the Queen, their eyes locked in a battle of wills. Markus pleaded for Isabella's release, vowing to do whatever it took to break the curse that held her captive.

The Snow Queen laughed, her icy breath forming frosty tendrils in the air.
"Love is but a fleeting emotion," she hissed.
"It is no match for the power of eternal winter."

With a wave of her hand, she summoned a blizzard of unyielding fury, aiming to eradicate Markus's defiance once and for all.

But Markus refused to yield. He summoned every ounce of love and determination within him, channelling it into a single act of self-sacrifice.

He stepped forward, offering himself as a sacrifice to save Isabella from the Snow Queen's clutches.

In that moment, love's true power manifested. Markus's act of pure selflessness shattered the Snow Queen's hold over Isabella.

The icy spell broke, and warmth flooded back into Isabella's heart, melting the ice that encased her soul.

With the Snow Queen's power weakened, Isabella and Markus fought together, using their love and unity to confront the Queen. In a climactic battle of fire and ice, they overpowered the Snow Queen, reducing her to a mere spectre of her former self.

As the Snow Queen's power waned, the eternal winter that had plagued the village slowly thawed. The warmth of love and hope returned, breathing life into the Once frozen hearts of the villagers.

Isabella and Markus stood as symbols of resilience and the transformative power of love. And so, in the aftermath of the Snow Queen's defeat, the villagers celebrated their newfound freedom, cherishing the love and warmth that had triumphed over the icy grip of darkness.

Isabella and Markus, forever bound by their shared ordeal, became the guiding light that led the village towards a future filled with hope and unity.

The tale of Isabella and the Snow Queen serves as a haunting reminder of the psychological warfare that can occur within the depths of the human mind.

It teaches us that true liberation comes from challenging our fears, embracing our inner strength, and reclaiming our own narrative.

Isabella's journey showcases the transformative potential of self-belief and the resilience of the human spirit in the face of psychological manipulation.

THE SHADOW

Once upon a time, in a forgotten corner of the world, there lived a man named Edgar. From a young age, Edgar was haunted by a peculiar shadow that clung to him like a malevolent spectre. It twisted and contorted, mimicking his every move, but never fully revealing itself.

As Edgar grew older, the shadow's presence grew more oppressive. It whispered in his ear, planting seeds of doubt and feeding his darkest fears.

It became a constant companion, a tormentor that twisted his perception of reality. Haunted by his shadow, Edgar's mind became a battlefield.

His thoughts were no longer his own, manipulated by the shadow's insidious influence. It painted a bleak portrait of his life, a tapestry of despair and self-loathing.

Every accomplishment was tarnished, every relationship poisoned by doubt. The shadow fed on Edgar's insecurities, weaving illusions that trapped him in a labyrinth of psychological torment.

It played with his senses, distorting his perceptions of time and space.

The boundary between reality and illusion blurred, and Edgar questioned his own sanity.

As the shadow's influence grew, Edgar's relationships with others deteriorated. The townspeople, fearful and ignorant, regarded him with suspicion and disdain.

They labelled him as cursed, a vessel of darkness. Their judgment fuelled the shadow's power, intensifying its grip on Edgar's fragile psyche.

Isolated and tormented, Edgar found solace in the darkest recesses of his mind. He descended further into a downward spiral, trapped within the labyrinthine corridors of his own thoughts.

The shadow's whispers grew louder, driving him to the brink of madness. But amidst the darkness, a glimmer of hope emerged.

A young woman named Adelaide, with her keen insight and empathetic nature, saw beyond the veil of Edgar's affliction. She recognized the shadow's hold on his psyche and vowed to free him from its clutches.

Adelaide delved deep into the forbidden arts of the mind, seeking ancient knowledge, and hidden remedies.

She learned of a mystical ritual said to banish malevolent shadows, a dangerous path paved with uncertainty. Undeterred, she embarked on a treacherous journey to acquire the ingredients and incantations necessary for the ritual.

As Adelaide returned to the town, she found Edgar sinking deeper into despair, his mind consumed by the shadow's relentless whispers.

With unwavering determination, she confronted the shadow head-on, her voice laced with conviction and compassion. She recited the ancient incantations, her words echoing through the night.

The shadows quivered; the air crackled with arcane energy. Adelaide's will clashed with the shadow's malevolence in a battle of psychic dominance.

In the depths of their psychic struggle, Edgar's consciousness became a battleground.

He witnessed fragments of his life, distorted, and manipulated by the shadow's influence. But as Adelaide's power surged, he found strength within himself, rising above the darkness that had ensnared him for so long.

With a final surge of energy, Adelaide banished the shadow, its form dissipating like smoke in the wind. Edgar gasped for air; his mind free from the shadow's suffocating grip.

The townspeople watched in awe, their fears replaced by wonder and gratitude. But the true horror of the shadow's influence lingered in Edgar's mind.

The psychological scars ran deep, and the battle to rebuild his shattered self-worth had just begun. With Adelaide's guidance, he embarked on a journey of healing, facing his demons and re-claiming his identity.

As the townspeople witnessed Edgar's transformation, they too began to question their own perceptions. The shadow's influence had extended beyond Edgar, spreading fear and judgment throughout the community.

They recognized the insidious nature of their own biases, and a collective desire for change took hold. The town underwent a profound shift, as compassion and understanding replaced judgment and fear.

The people, united by their shared experiences, forged a community of empathy and acceptance.

They pledged to confront their own shadows, both metaphorical and literal, and to support one another in their ongoing battles. However, even with the shadow banished, the scars of Edgar's psychological torment remained.

Nightmares plagued his sleep, and anxiety clouded his waking hours. The battle against the shadow had taken a toll on his mental well-being, and the journey to heal his fractured psyche would be a long and arduous one.

Through Adelaide's guidance, Edgar confronted his deepest fears and overcame the shadow's influence. However, the journey to heal his fractured psyche was far from over.

The scars of the shadow's torment ran deep, manifesting in haunting nightmares and debilitating anxiety.

In his quest for healing, Edgar sought the aid of healers, therapists, and support groups.

He delved into the depths of his subconscious, unravelling the layers of trauma, and rebuilding his shattered self-worth.

Through introspection and self-reflection, he confronted the root causes of his vulnerability to the shadow's influence, uncovering buried pain and addressing unresolved emotional wounds.

Yet, even as he progressed on his path to recovery, the shadow's whispers lingered in the darkest corners of Edgar's mind. Its haunting voice echoed in his dreams, a constant reminder of the psychological battle he had fought.

But Edgar refused to let the shadow regain its hold.

With each passing day, Edgar grew stronger. He learned to recognize the shadow's deceitful tactics and developed strategies to challenge its grip on his thoughts. He practiced self-compassion, nurturing a sense of self-worth that no longer relied on external validation.

As Edgar shared his story with others who had faced similar battles, he discovered the power of connection and empathy.

Together, they formed a support network, a sanctuary of understanding and acceptance. They shared their experiences, providing solace and encouragement to one another on their paths to healing.

Through therapy, artistic expression, and introspection, Edgar learned to confront his deepest fears head-on. He faced the darkest corners of his psyche, embracing the wounds that had once held him captive.
In doing so, he unravelled the intricate web of psychological manipulation woven by the shadow, reclaiming his own narrative.

In the annals of psychological horror, the tale of Edgar and the shadow stands as a testament to the transformative power of self-awareness, self-compassion, and human connection.

It encourages us to confront our own inner demons, to seek support and healing, and to never underestimate the strength of the human spirit in the face of psychological adversity.

THE STORY OF THE KINGS SON

Once upon a time, in a kingdom shrouded in darkness, there lived a young prince named Victor. The kingdom was ruled by his father, a tyrannical king whose heart was consumed by greed and power.

Under the king's oppressive reign, the people suffered, their hopes and dreams extinguished like flickering
candles in the night.

Victor, burdened by the weight of his father's legacy, felt suffocated within the confines of the palace walls.

The whispers of the tormented souls echoed through the corridors, a haunting reminder of the king's ruthless reign. Yet, amidst the chaos and despair, a spark of rebellion ignited within Victor's heart.

Driven by an insatiable thirst for freedom, Victor embarked on a perilous journey to uncover the truth behind his father's tyranny.

He ventured beyond the castle walls, traversing treacherous landscapes, and delving into forbidden realms where secrets were whispered among the shadows.

As he journeyed deeper into the unknown, Victor felt the weight of the kingdom's suffering pressing upon his soul.

The people's anguish permeated the very air, their hopes and dreams shattered by the relentless grip of his father's tyranny. Victor resolved to free them from this oppressive reign, no matter the cost.

In his quest for truth, Victor stumbled upon a forgotten chamber concealed within the palace. Within its depths, he discovered an ancient manuscript, its pages adorned with cryptic symbols and dark illustrations.

As he deciphered the arcane text, he unravelled a chilling tale of corruption, deceit, and a sinister pact forged by his father.

The story revealed that the king's ascent to power had come at a grave cost.

Desperate to maintain his dominion, the king had made a pact with a malevolent entity, selling his soul in exchange for boundless power.

This dark presence, unseen by the people, cast a malevolent shadow over the entire kingdom, feeding off the misery and despair it engendered.

Victor's heart sank as he realized the full extent of his father's wickedness. The people's suffering, the shattered dreams, and the oppressive atmosphere were all orchestrated by this malevolent force lurking within the shadows.

Determined to break this cycle of despair, Victor vowed to confront the malevolent entity and free his kingdom from its clutches.

As Victor delved deeper into the kingdom's darkness, the malevolent entity fought back, sensing the threat to its dominion.

It toyed with Victor's mind, unleashing twisted illusions and haunting night-mares. The prince's sanity teetered on the edge as he struggled to distinguish reality from the malevolent entity's insidious machinations.

In the depths of his psychological battle, Victor encountered the ghosts of those who had fallen victim to his father's cruelty. Their tormented souls cried out for justice, their pain searing through his consciousness.

Their collective voices merged into a cacophony of anguish, fuelling Victor's determination to liberate them from the clutches of this malevolent force.

Through his journey, Victor encountered allies who had also suffered at the hands of his father. Together, they formed a formidable resistance, united in their quest to eradicate the darkness that had plagued the kingdom for far too long.

Their shared experiences strengthened their resolve, as they pooled their knowledge and resources to confront the malevolent entity.

With every step closer to the entity's lair, Victor felt the weight of its influence growing stronger. The very air seemed to thicken with malevolence, suffocating his spirit. Yet, fuelled by his determination and the camaraderie of his allies, he pressed on, determined to confront the entity head-on.

In a climactic battle between light and darkness, truth and deceit, Victor faced the malevolent entity with unyielding resolve.

The entity, its form twisted and grotesque, unleashed its full wrath upon him. Illusions danced before Victor's eyes, distorting his perceptions, and testing the limits of his sanity.

But Victor refused to succumb to the entity's insidious influence. He summoned the strength within himself, drawing upon the collective power of his allies and the resilience of the people he sought to liberate.

With every ounce of his being, he channelled his rage, his pain, and his determination into a final, decisive blow. As the malevolent entity dissipated into the void, its influence over the kingdom shattered like a broken mirror.

The people, awakened from their collective nightmare, emerged from the shadows with a newfound sense of hope.

Victor, hailed as the hero who had liberated them from the clutches of darkness, assumed the mantle of leadership, vowing to rebuild the realm on foundations of justice and compassion.

However, the psychological scars of the kingdom's dark past ran deep. Victor, haunted by his encounters with the malevolent entity, bore the weight of the kingdom's suffering upon his shoulders.

Nightmares plagued his sleep, and the remnants of the entity's influence echoed in his thoughts.

But Victor remained resolute. He sought solace and guidance from wise mentors and healers, delving into the depths of his own psyche to confront the residual trauma.

Through introspection and self-reflection, he unravelled the tangled web of psychological torment, reclaiming his identity and forging a path toward healing.

The tale of Victor and the malevolent entity stands as a chilling reminder of the power of psychological manipulation and the enduring strength of the human spirit.

It serves as a cautionary tale, highlighting the dangers of unchecked power and the importance of empathy, unity, and the pursuit of truth.

BLUEBEARD (GILLES DE RAIS)

Deep in the heart of the sinister countryside, there stood a foreboding mansion. Its walls were shrouded in mystery, its halls echoing with secrets that chilled the soul.

This was the residence of Lord Lucien, a man known throughout the land as Bluebeard.

Bluebeard, with his enigmatic charm and wealth, had lured many women into his lair, only for them to vanish without a trace. The people whispered tales of his malevolence, of the blood that stained his hands and the darkness that consumed his soul.

Yet, despite the warnings, curiosity beckoned to those who dared to venture close. Among the villagers was a young woman named Isabella. Her beauty and grace captivated the hearts of many, but her spirit of adventure led her to the doorstep of Bluebeard's mansion.

The allure of forbidden knowledge and the promise of an opulent life drew her in, blinding her to the danger that lurked within.

Isabella became Bluebeard's wife, the mistress of his grand estate. At first, the mansion appeared to be a paradise of luxury and opulence, but a sense of unease gnawed at Isabella's core.

The rooms were adorned with priceless treasures, but their beauty was tainted by an oppressive atmosphere, a dark-ness that clung to the air like a poisonous mist.

As time went on, Isabella's curiosity grew, and she found herself compelled to explore the mansion's forbidden chambers. Ignoring the warnings of Bluebeard, she ventured into the depths of his secrets. Behind each door, she discovered a horrifying truth a room filled with bloodstained garments, a chamber of torture devices, a gallery of portraits depicting Bluebeard's former wives, frozen in eternal agony.

The horrors she witnessed seeped into Isabella's soul, poisoning her mind with a chilling realization.

Bluebeard, the man she had vowed to love and honour, was a monster a sadistic predator who revelled in the suffering of his victims.

The weight of this knowledge bore down upon her, crushing her spirit with the suffocating grip of fear.

Haunted by the spectre's of Bluebeard's past, Isabella's sanity teetered on the brink of collapse.

Nightmares plagued her sleep, vivid visions of the tortured souls trapped within the mansion's walls.

The whispers of the dead echoed through her mind, their anguished cries filling her ears even in the waking hours.

The psychological torment intensified as Bluebeard's hold over Isabella tightened. He grew suspicious of her curiosity, sensing her growing awareness of his true nature. With each passing day, his affection transformed into possessiveness and control, suffocating Isabella's spirit.

She became a prisoner within her own home, trapped in a gilded cage from which escape seemed impossible.

But deep within Isabella's shattered psyche, a spark of resistance ignited. She yearned for freedom, to break the chains of her captivity and expose Bluebeard's malevolence to the world.

Gathering her strength, she plotted her escape, seeking allies among the mansion's staff, who had long been silenced by fear. Together, they devised a plan to expose Bluebeard's crimes and bring him to justice.

Isabella's resolve burned like a wildfire, fuelled by the horrors she had witnessed and the torment she had endured.

The day of reckoning drew near, as Isabella prepared to face her captor and reveal his true nature to the world.

The confrontation with Bluebeard was a clash of wills, a battle between light and darkness. Isabella, armed with the knowledge of his crimes, stood before him, her voice steady and unwavering.

She ex-posed his monstrous acts to the world, revealing the true face of the man who had tormented and killed countless innocent women.

In a fit of rage, Bluebeard lunged at Isabella, his fury unleashed upon her. But she, fuelled by her newfound strength and the support of those who had rallied to her cause, fought back with unwavering determination.

The mansion became a battleground, a cacophony of violence and desperation. The struggle reached its climax as Isabella delivered a final, decisive blow.

Bluebeard, defeated and exposed, lay lifeless on the cold marble floor.

The mansion, once a symbol of terror and darkness, fell silent.

The weight of its secrets lifted, dissipating into the air like a fading nightmare.

Isabella, battered and scarred, emerged from the mansion's depths, a survivor of the horrors that had threatened to consume her.

The villagers, once fearful and under Bluebeard's spell, saw her as a hero a symbol of courage and resilience.

The psychological effect of Bluebeard's manipulation on Isabella is a central theme of the story. His calculated control over her thoughts and emotions gradually erodes her sense of self, leaving her trapped in a web of fear and uncertainty.

Isabella's journey through the dark recesses of the mansion mirrors her descent into madness as she confronts the twisted truth of her husband's nature.

The terror that Isabella experiences is not limited to physical threats but extends into the realm of psychological warfare.

Bluebeard's manipulation plays on her deepest fears and insecurities, exploiting her vulnerabilities to maintain his power over her.

The constant state of unease and the haunting images that fill Isabella's mind create a suffocating atmosphere of psychological horror.

As the story unfolds, Isabella's determination to break free from Bluebeard's control becomes a beacon of hope.

Her journey from victim to survivor is marked by moments of resilience and defiance.

She finds strength in her will to expose the truth, rallying allies who share her desire for justice.

The climactic confrontation between Isabella and Bluebeard is a battle not only of physical strength but also of psychological fortitude.

Isabella's unwavering resolve to confront her captor and reveal his monstrous deeds is a testament to the indomitable nature of the human spirit.

Ultimately, the story serves as a cautionary tale, reminding us of the horrors that can lurk behind closed doors and masked faces. It calls us to remain vigilant, to trust our instincts, and to confront the darkness that resides both within ourselves and in the world around us.

he tale of Isabella and Bluebeard serves as a chilling testament to the power of psychological horror. It delves into the depths of the human psyche, exploring the fragility of the mind when faced with unspeakable evil.

Through Isabella's harrowing journey, we are reminded that true horror often lies not in the physical acts of violence but in the psychological torment inflicted upon the innocent.

THE GLASS COFFIN

Once upon a time, in a small village nestled in the heart of a dense forest, there lived a young woman named Eliza.

She was known for her unparalleled beauty, with cascading golden locks and eyes that sparkled like the stars. But behind her captivating exterior lay a troubled soul, haunted by the darkness that resided within.

One fateful day, as Eliza was wandering through the forest, she stumbled upon a peculiar sight. In a hidden clearing, surrounded by an enchanting array of wildflowers, lay a glass coffin.

Inside rested a young man, his features frozen in an eternal slumber. The villagers whispered tales of his tragic fate a prince cursed to sleep indefinitely until a true love's kiss could awaken him.

Intrigued by the mysterious presence of the glass coffin, Eliza approached cautiously. The pale, lifeless face of the prince stirred something within her—a curiosity and longing she could not ignore.

Without hesitation, she pressed her lips against his, hoping to break the curse that held him captive.

But as her lips touched his, an icy chill engulfed her. The prince's eyes fluttered open, revealing an empty gaze that sent shivers down Eliza's spine.

The curse had been broken, but it seemed that something far more sinister had awakened alongside the prince.

From that moment on, Eliza's life took a twisted turn. The once peaceful village became plagued by nightmares and inexplicable misfortunes. Eliza found herself tormented by visions of darkness and despair, her mind a battleground of fragmented memories and unsettling thoughts.

The townspeople grew fearful of Eliza, believing her to be the harbinger of the prince's curse. They shunned her, casting her out as an outcast, blaming her for their suffering.

Eliza, trapped in a web of guilt and isolation, became a prisoner of her own mind.

Deep within Eliza's psyche, a psychological battle raged on, mirroring the external horrors she faced.

The curse of the glass coffin had not only awakened the darkness within the prince but had also unleashed Eliza's own inner demons.

She found herself caught in a twisted dance between her own fears, insecurities, and the malevolent presence of the prince.

The psychological torment she endured manifested in various forms.

Nightmares plagued her sleep, vivid and visceral, where she was trapped in a never-ending loop of terror.

Each night brought forth new horrors, her mind creating scenarios that reflected her deepest fears and anxieties. She became a prisoner within her own dreams, unable to find solace even in the realm of slumber.

During her waking hours, Eliza's perception of reality began to blur. The line between what was real and what was imagined grew increasingly thin.

Shadows seemed to whisper secrets to her, objects distorted and shifted before her eyes, and the voices of the villagers echoed in her mind, their accusatory words intertwining with her own self-doubt.

The psychological effect of the villagers' rejection and persecution weighed heavily on Eliza's fragile psyche.

Their belief in her malevolence fed her own insecurities, amplifying her feelings of guilt and isolation.

She questioned her own worth, tortured by the notion that perhaps the darkness within her was indeed real and that she was undeserving of love and acceptance.

Yet, amidst the darkness, a glimmer of resilience flickered within Eliza. She fought against the invasive thoughts, the relentless whispers of doubt and self-loathing.

She sought refuge in her own strength, determined to break free from the psychological prison that held her captive.

As the days turned into nights, Eliza's psychological torment intensified. The presence of the prince loomed over her every thought, his empty gaze following her wherever she went.

She became trapped in a waking nightmare, unable to escape the clutches of her own mind.

Desperate for answers, Eliza sought solace in the remnants of an ancient book, hidden deep within the village library. Its pages revealed the dark history of the glass coffin a tale of a prince who had fallen victim to a malevolent enchantress.

The curse that had held him captive reflected the torment he had inflicted upon others in his former life.

Eliza realized that she had unknowingly awakened not only the prince but also the darkness that had consumed him.

The curse had transferred to her, and now she bore the weight of his sins.

The glass coffin had become a prison, a symbol of her entrapment in a psychological abyss.

Haunted by the prince's malevolence, Eliza's mind teetered on the edge of madness.

The lines between reality and illusion blurred as she confronted her own demons, forced to reckon with the darkness that resided within her.

The village became a twisted playground, each resident a distorted reflection of her own fears and insecurities.

To confront the darkness within, Eliza delved into her own subconscious, exploring the hidden recesses of her mind. In this journey of self-discovery, she encountered fragments of memories, long forgotten traumas, and unresolved emotions. T

he psychological battle took on a new dimension as Eliza faced her own personal demons, forced to confront the pain and darkness that had shaped her.

The presence of the prince, though a symbol of malevolence, became a catalyst for Eliza's inner exploration.

She recognized the parallels between his curse and her own struggles, understanding that the darkness within her was not inherently evil but a part of her own human experience.

Through introspection and self-acceptance, she sought to integrate the shadow aspects of her psyche, trans-forming her pain into a source of strength.

As Eliza unravelled the intricate layers of her psyche, she gradually reclaimed her power. She confronted the prince's malevolence within herself, acknowledging the capacity for darkness that resided within her own soul.

In this cathartic confrontation, she dismantled the psychological hold he had over her, liberating herself from the shackles of guilt and fear.

The psychological journey was not without its setbacks. Eliza encountered moments of despair and doubt, the weight of her own psyche threatening to consume her.

But with each hurdle, she grew stronger, forging an unbreakable resolve to face her fears and rewrite the narrative of her own existence.

As her psychological battle waged on, Eliza's grip on sanity slipped further.

The villagers, consumed by their own paranoia and fuelled by their belief in her malevolence, turned against her.

They hunted her like a wild beast, determined to rid themselves of the curse she bore.

In the depths of her despair, Eliza made a choice—a choice to embrace the darkness within and con-front the prince's malevolence head-on.

She sought out the enchantress, the source of the curse, and confronted her with a fiery determination.

In a climactic battle of wills, Eliza reclaimed her power, breaking free from the cycle of torment and despair.

As the village returned to its former tranquillity, Eliza emerged from the shadows, forever changed by her harrowing ordeal. She carried the scars of her psychological battle, a reminder of the strength she had found within herself.

The glass coffin, once a symbol of her entrapment, shattered into a thousand shards, each one representing her resilience and triumph over darkness.

Through Eliza's journey, we are reminded of the fragility of the human psyche and the strength required to confront our own demons.

It serves as a cautionary tale, urging us to acknowledge and confront the darkness that resides within us, for it is only through facing our fears that we can find true liberation.

And so, the tale of Eliza and the glass coffin becomes a haunting testament to the indomitable nature of the human spirit and the transformative power of self-acceptance.

In the realm of psychological horror, it stands as a testament to the resilience and triumph of the human mind.

THE SNOWMAN

Once upon a time, in a small village nestled amidst snow-covered mountains, lived a young woman named Amelia. The village was renowned for its icy winters, where the snowfall was heavy and relentless.

But amidst the beauty of the winter wonderland, a chilling tale lingered a tale of a cursed snow-man that brought terror to the villagers.

Amelia, an artist known for her skilful craftsmanship, was captivated by the mysterious legend of the snowman. Intrigued by the tales of its malevolent presence, she set out to create her own master piece snowman that would stand as a testament to her artistic prowess.

With nimble hands and a creative mind, Amelia shaped the snowman into an imposing figure, adorned with an eerie grin and piercing eyes that seemed to penetrate the soul.

As she finished sculpting the final details, she couldn't help but feel a strange connection to her creation a connection that would plunge her into a harrowing psychological journey.

As night fell upon the village, Amelia noticed an unsettling change in the atmosphere. The snowfall grew heavier, and an icy breeze whispered through the trees.

The villagers retreated into their homes, fearful of the legendary snowman and the dark powers it possessed.

But Amelia, drawn to the allure of her creation, couldn't resist the temptation to witness the snow-man's transformation first-hand. As she stepped outside, the snowman came alive before her eyes.

It moved with an unnatural grace, its coal eyes fixed on her, sending a shiver down her spine. Intrigued and enticed, Amelia followed the snowman through the wintry landscape.

It led her deep into the heart of the forest, where an ancient curse had long held sway. The forest was a realm of twisted shadows, where the line between reality and illusion blurred, and the mind played tricks on the senses.

Amelia's psychological journey had begun, a descent into the depths of her own psyche.

The snowman, a manifestation of her own desires and fears, became her guide through the labyrinth of her mind.

Each step brought her closer to confronting her own darkness and the psychological demons that had plagued her for years.

As Amelia delved deeper into the psychological labyrinth, she encountered a series of surreal and disorienting experiences that tested the very fabric of her sanity.

The labyrinth seemed to morph and shift, its walls pulsating with an eerie energy, constantly reshaping itself to mirror the twists and turns of her own mind.

In one chamber of the labyrinth, Amelia found herself in a haunting recreation of her childhood home. Memories long buried resurfaced with a vengeance, casting a dark shadow over her psyche.

She relived moments of fear, neglect, and emotional abuse, the echoes of which had lingered within her subconscious for years. The labyrinth played tricks on Amelia's senses, distorting her perception of time and space.

She would find herself trapped in never-ending corridors that seemed to stretch on infinitely, unable to find an escape.

The walls whispered secrets, their voices a cacophony of doubts and insecurities, threatening to engulf her in a sea of self-doubt.

In another chamber, Amelia encountered the fractured fragments of her identity. She confronted different versions of herself, each representing a different aspect of her personality.

The optimistic and confident Amelia clashed with the timid and self-conscious one, their internal battles raging within her psyche.

It became a battle for dominance, as she struggled to reconcile her conflicting thoughts and emotions.

The labyrinth also presented Amelia with surreal visions and symbolic encounters. She came face to face with anthropomorphic creatures that personified her deepest fears and desires.

The Raven of Regret taunted her with reminders of past mistakes, while the Serpent of Temptation enticed her with promises of false gratification.

These encounters forced her to confront her own vulnerabilities and confront the darker aspects of her nature.

Throughout her journey, Amelia faced a relentless barrage of self-doubt and negative self-talk. The labyrinth exploited her insecurities, amplifying her inner critic to unbearable levels.

Voices whispered in her ear, mocking her worth and casting doubt on her abilities. She was forced to confront the deeply ingrained beliefs that held her back and embrace her own inherent strength and resilience.

Yet, amid the psychological chaos, glimmers of hope and self-discovery emerged. Amelia stumbled upon hidden chambers within the labyrinth that housed fragments of forgotten dreams and aspirations.

She rediscovered her love for art, embracing the therapeutic power of creativity as a means to navigate the labyrinth and reclaim her sense of self.

In the darkest corners of the labyrinth, Amelia encountered manifestations of the traumas that had haunted her for so long. She faced the Spectres of her past, the shadows of pain and loss that had cast a long shadow over her life.

These encounters were excruciatingly painful, requiring her to summon every ounce of courage to confront the ghosts that haunted her.

As she progressed through the labyrinth, Amelia began to unravel the interconnected threads of her psyche.

She recognized that the labyrinth reflected her own internal struggles, a manifestation of the psychological barriers she had erected to protect herself from further pain.

It was a journey of self-discovery and healing, a gradual unravelling of the layers that had concealed her true self.

In the heart of the labyrinth, Amelia faced the ultimate test of her psychological strength. She stood before a towering mirror that reflected her true essence, her deepest fears, and her most profound desires.

The mirror compelled her to confront her own reflection, to acknowledge her flaws and embrace her inherent worthiness.

With each step forward, Amelia reclaimed a piece of herself, shattering the illusion of the labyrinth's power over her. She learned to silence the voices of self-doubt and embrace self-compassion.

The psychological labyrinth became a conduit for her transformation, a crucible through which she emerged stronger, more self-aware, and empowered.

But the snowman, a personification of her own fears and insecurities, remained a formidable adversary.

It tested her resolve, tempting her to succumb to the allure of darkness, to embrace the madness that threatened to consume her. Amelia had to make a choice a choice between succumbing to the darkness or finding the strength to reclaim her sanity.

In a climactic battle within the recesses of her own mind, Amelia confronted the snowman.

With every ounce of her will, she fought against the malevolent presence, dismantling the illusions it had woven and shattering the chains of its psychological hold.

n that moment, she reclaimed her power, emerging as a survivor, forever changed by her psychological journey.

As the sun rose over the village, the snow-man melted into oblivion, leaving no trace of its presence except for the indelible mark it had left on Amelia's psyche.

The village, once paralyzed by fear, gradually regained its tranquillity. The legend of the cursed snowman became a cautionary tale a reminder of the power of the mind and the resilience of the human spirit.

Amelia, forever marked by her psychological odyssey, emerged as a testament to the triumph of the human psyche over darkness.

She carried with her the scars of her journey, a reminder of the strength she had found within herself.

The psychological labyrinth she had navigated had transformed her, illuminating the darkest corners of her mind, and setting her free from the chains of her past.

The tale of Amelia and the snowman serves as a chilling exploration of the depths of the human psyche.

It delves into the intricacies of psychological horror, examining the fragile boundaries between reality and illusion, and the power of the mind to shape one's perception of the world.

The psychological labyrinth that Amelia navigated serves as a metaphor for the complexity of the human mind and the challenges we face in confronting our own inner demons.

It reminds us that the path to self-discovery and healing is often fraught with uncertainty and darkness.

Yet, through perseverance and self-acceptance, we can emerge from the labyrinth of our own minds stronger and more resilient.

"In the face of adversity, our spirits are tested, but our resilience prevails. We are survivors, warriors who have weathered the storms of psychological trauma. From the depths of darkness, we rise, stronger and more determined than ever. Our scars bear witness to our strength, and our hearts, once shattered, now beat with renewed purpose. We embrace our past as part of our journey, knowing that our survival is a testament to our indomitable spirit."

Quote by Angeless Watkins-Gallar

THE DARK SECRETS OF FAIRY TALES
ACT 4

Riquet of the Tuft (Ricky of the Tuft)

In a time long ago, there was a young woman named Isabella. Born into a noble family, she possessed beauty that surpassed all others in the land.

But beneath her stunning exterior, there lay a darkness that consumed her soul a darkness born from a childhood of neglect and emotional abuse.

Isabella grew up in a lavish mansion, surrounded by opulence and servants who attended to her every need. However, her parents were distant and cold, showing her little affection or attention.

Instead, they focused on their own desires and ambitions, leaving Isabella feeling invisible and unloved.

As the years passed, Isabella 's heart grew heavy with the weight of her parents' indifference.

She sought sol-ace in the sprawling gardens surrounding the mansion, finding comfort in the delicate flowers, and whispering trees.

It was there that she first encountered Ricky, a peculiar creature with wild tufts of hair and piercing eyes.

Ricky, despite his unconventional appearance, exuded an air of confidence and wisdom. He saw through the façade of Isabella 's perfect life, recognizing the deep pain hidden beneath her beautiful exterior.

Intrigued by her sadness, he offered her a deal a chance to escape her stifling existence and embark on a journey of self-discovery.

Driven by a desperate longing for freedom and belonging, Isabella agreed to Ricky's proposition. With a touch of his hand, he transported her to a world beyond her wildest imagination a world where darkness and desire intertwined, where the boundaries of reality blurred, and the true nature of her soul was laid bare.

As Isabella delved deeper into the psychological labyrinth, the true nature of Ricky, the enigmatic guide, began to reveal itself in more sinister and unsettling ways.

His once beguiling appearance morphed into something more nightmarish, an embodiment of the twisted depths of the human psyche.

His wild tufts of hair grew longer and more unkempt, resembling dark tendrils that seemed to writhe and move of their own accord.

His piercing eyes, once filled with wisdom, now held a cold, predatory gaze that sent shivers down Isabella 's spine.

It was as if Ricky had shed his façade of benevolence, revealing his true form a manipulative entity that thrived on the vulnerability of the human mind.

Ricky's words carried a hypnotic power, weaving through Isabella 's thoughts and exploiting her deepest insecurities.

He preyed on her yearning for love and acceptance, using it as a weapon to twist her mind and steer her further into the labyrinth's psychological traps.

His voice, once comforting, now dripped with a sinister undertone that echoed through the darkest corners of her psyche.

As Isabella confronted her fragmented memories and encountered the distorted reflections of herself, Ricky's influence grew stronger. He played with her perceptions, distorting her sense of reality, and blurring the line between truth and illusion.

His manipulations seeped into her thoughts, planting seeds of doubt and paranoia that festered and grew with each passing trial.

Ricky revelled in the chaos he wrought upon Isabella 's mind. He whispered twisted notions, convincing her that her pain was her own doing, that she was unworthy of love and destined for a life of isolation and despair.

The more Isabella fought against his manipulations, the more viciously he tightened his grip, driving her deeper into the labyrinth of her own self-doubt.

Isabella 's mind became a battleground, with Ricky as the puppeteer pulling the strings. He exploited her fears, magnifying them until they consumed her every thought. He twisted her perception of reality, distorting memories and blurring the lines between past and present.

It was a psychological dance of torment, as Ricky revelled in his power to unravel her fragile psyche. As Isabella ventured deeper into the psychological labyrinth, the tendrils of her parents' emotional neglect tightened around her psyche.

The labyrinth itself seemed to reflect the echoes of her childhood, with each twist and turn representing a different facet of the love she had been denied.

The more Isabella fought against his manipulations, the more viciously he tightened his grip, driving her deeper into the labyrinth of her own self-doubt.

Isabella 's mind became a battleground, with Ricky as the puppeteer pulling the strings. He exploited her fears, magnifying them until they consumed her every thought. He twisted her perception of reality, distorting memories and blurring the lines between past and present.

It was a psychological dance of torment, as Ricky revelled in his power to unravel her fragile psyche.

As Isabella ventured deeper into the psychological labyrinth, the tendrils of her parents' emotional neglect tightened around her psyche.

The labyrinth itself seemed to reflect the echoes of her childhood, with each twist and turn representing a different facet of the love she had been denied.

In one corridor of the labyrinth, Isabella found herself in a hauntingly empty room, devoid of any warmth or affection. The walls were adorned with portraits of happy families, their joy serving as a stark contrast to her own reality.

The silence of the room echoed with the unspoken words of love that had never been uttered, leaving Isabella feeling like a mere shadow in a world of vibrant emotions.

As she navigated the labyrinth's winding paths, Isabella encountered fragmented memories that had been buried deep within her subconscious. She saw herself as a young child, reaching out for her parents' attention, only to be met with indifference and dismissive gestures.

Each memory brought with it a wave of pain and longing, the wounds of neglect reopened and raw.

The labyrinth played tricks on Isabella 's mind, distorting her perceptions, and intensifying her yearning for love.

She would catch glimpses of fleeting moments when her parents could have shown affection, only to have those moments cruelly snatched away.

It was as if the labyrinth itself conspired to torment her, twisting her longing into a desperate hunger for validation.

The labyrinth amplified Isabella's need for affection, heightening her desperation to fill the void left by her parents' emotional absence.

It toyed with her emotions, distorting her perception of love, and blurring the line between genuine affection and manipulation. It became a treacherous dance, as Isabella sought solace in fleeting moments of connection, only to be plunged into deeper despair when they proved fleeting.

As she continued her harrowing journey, Isabella found herself standing at the threshold of a forbidden chamber within the labyrinth a chamber that held the key to her liberation.

Inside, she confronted an embodiment of her parents' neglect, a monstrous figure that loomed over her with a chilling aura of indifference. With trembling resolve, Isabella faced the figure head-on, her voice quivering but firm. She unleashed a torrent of emotions, pouring out years of unspoken pain and longing.

The figure's stoic façade cracked, revealing a flicker of remorse, but it was too late. Isabella had found her voice, reclaiming the power that had been stolen from her.

As she confronted the embodiment of her parents' neglect, Isabella realized that their emotional absence had never been her fault.

She had carried the weight of their indifference for far too long, but in that moment of confrontation, she relinquished it.

Amidst the psychological chaos, Isabella began to question Ricky's true nature.

Was he a benevolent guide leading her to self-discovery, or a malevolent entity intent on manipulating her for his own twisted pleasure?

The boundaries between friend and foe blurred, leaving her in a state of constant unease and suspicion.

Yet, Ricky's influence held a powerful allure that was difficult to resist. He offered Isabella a tantalizing glimpse of the freedom and validation she so desperately craved, even if it came at the cost of her own sanity.

The psychological labyrinth became a prison of her own making, as Ricky exploited her vulnerabilities and manipulated her desires.

In the final confrontation, as Isabella faced the embodiment of her parents' neglect, she found herself at a crossroads.

The darkness of Ricky's influence loomed large, threatening to consume her entirely. But in a moment of clarity, she recognized the insidious nature of his manipulations.

With a surge of inner strength, she defied Ricky's hold, reclaiming her own mind and breaking free from his psychological grasp.

As the labyrinth crumbled around her, Isabella emerged with scars that would forever mark her psyche. The battle with Ricky had left its indelible imprint, but she had found her own truth amidst the chaos.

No longer would she allow herself to be controlled by external forces, be they her parents' neglect or Ricky's manipulations.

As the realm of the psychological horror faded away, Isabella found herself back in the familiar gardens surrounding her childhood home. The mansion stood before her, unchanged, but she saw it through new eyes, eyes that no longer sought validation or approval.

She had reclaimed her sense of self, breaking free from the chains that had bound her for so long.

Her journey through the realm of psychological horror had transformed her, leaving an indelible mark on her soul. She had learned that true beauty lay not in physical appearance, but in the strength to confront one's own demons and embrace the complexities of the human psyche.

In the realm of adult psychological horror, the tale of Isabella and Ricky stands as a testament to the resilience of the human spirit and the transformative power of self-acceptance.

It urges us to confront our own psychological battles, to explore the depths of our own minds, and to emerge from the dark-ness with newfound strength and self-love.

THE MASTER CAT (PUSS IN BOOTS)

Once upon a time, in a world plagued by shadows and deception, there existed a cunning and enigmatic feline named Puck.

With emerald eyes that gleamed with an unsettling intelligence and a smile that concealed untold secrets, Puck roamed the land, seeking out those whose hearts were consumed by darkness.

In a small village nestled deep within the forest, there lived a, there lived a down-on-his-luck miller named Jacob.

Burdened by debt and despair, shunned by the villagers for his peculiar abilities and haunted by a tragic past. His parents, driven by fear and ignorance, had abandoned him in the woods as a child, leaving him to fend for himself.

From that day forward, Jacob's life was marked by loneliness and a deep yearning for connection.

Jacob had always possessed an uncanny affinity for animals. From the tiniest insects to the largest predators, she could communicate with them effortlessly.

They became her only companions, the only beings who understood her and offered solace in a world that rejected him.

One fateful day, as Jacob wandered through the woods, he stumbled upon a peculiar cat with shimmering black fur. Its eyes bore a striking resemblance to emerald jewels, glinting with a mix of mischief and wisdom.

Intrigued by the cat's presence, Jacob cautiously approached, drawn in by an invisible force that seemed to pull her towards it.

The cat introduced itself as Puck, a creature of ancient knowledge and mystical power. It claimed to have the ability to grant Jacob the one thing she desired above all else a place where he belonged, where his powers would be celebrated rather than feared.

With a seductive purr, Puck made an offer that Jacob couldn't resist.

"If you follow me, Jacob, I will lead you to a realm where your abilities will be cherished," Puck purred, his eyes glinting with mischief.

"But there is a price to pay."

Driven by desperation and a longing for acceptance, Jacob agreed without hesitation. Little did he know that Puck's promises came with a hefty cost an unbreakable bond that would forever bind him to his will.

Jacob had unknowingly become a pawn in Puck's intricate game of manipulation and deceit.

Under Puck's guidance, Jacob was transformed into a dashing figure, clothed in fine garments that concealed the chains that now bound him. Puck's power was not limited to mere appearances; he granted Jacob the ability to communicate with animals, a gift that would prove both a blessing and a curse.

With Puck's whispered instructions, Jacob embarked on a mission to deceive and manipulate the unsuspecting townsfolk. He charmed his way into the homes and hearts of the wealthy, playing the role of a charismatic and charming nobleman.

But behind the façade, Jacob was tormented by the knowledge of his servitude to Puck, his every action dictated by the enigmatic feline's whims.

As Jacob delved deeper into his deceptions, he found himself drawn to the darkest corners of human nature.

The power he wielded over others fed a hunger within him, a hunger for control and dominance. The once-humble miller revelled in his newfound influence, savouring the fear and adulation that his manipulations elicited.

As they journeyed deeper into the heart of the forest, Jacob's world transformed before his eyes.

The once familiar trees twisted and contorted, their branches resembling gnarled claws reaching out to ensnare him.

The air grew thick with an oppressive darkness, and whispers echoed through the shadows, filling Jacob's mind with doubt and confusion.

But as the web of deceit grew ever more intricate, cracks began to form in Jacob's carefully constructed façade. His grip on reality wavered, as he questioned his own identity and struggled to differentiate between truth and illusion.

Puck's influence seeped into his psyche, distorting his perceptions, and driving him further into a labyrinth of psychological torment.

Haunted by guilt and plagued by nightmares, Jacob's mind became a battlefield, torn between his de-sire for freedom and the ever-tightening grip of Puck's control.

He was trapped, a pawn in a game that he had unwittingly entered, his every move dictated by the whims of a malevolent feline.

As Jacob's torment escalated, he found solace in the company of a mysterious young woman named Emily.

With eyes as deep and dark as the night sky, and a spirit that seemed to burn with an inner fire, Emily became Jacob's tether to reality.

In her presence, he felt a glimmer of hope, a respite from the suffocating grip of Puck's influence. Jacob and Evelyn stood before Puck, their eyes burning with determination.

They had endured endless psychological torment, their minds twisted and toyed with by the malevolent cat.

But now, they were ready to face him head-on, to challenge his power and reclaim their freedom.

As they locked eyes with Puck, a wave of intense energy surged through their bodies.

They could feel the weight of their past pain, the scars of their psychological battles, fuelling their re-solve. Their inner strength, forged through the darkest of times, surged forth like a raging storm.

With a primal scream, Jacob and Evelyn unleashed their pent-up fury, their minds reaching a heightened state of awareness. They tapped into the depths of their resilience, drawing upon the indomitable spirit that had carried them through their personal hells.

In that moment, they became unstoppable forces, unyielding in their pursuit of liberation.

Puck's eyes widened as he sensed the shift in power. The confident smirk that had adorned his face wavered for the first time, replaced by a flicker of doubt.

He had underestimated the strength of these two souls, their resilience proving to be a formidable adversary.

Jacob and Evelyn advanced toward Puck, their steps steady and purposeful.

They could hear his voice, dripping with malice, whispering venomous lies into their minds, attempting to sow seeds of doubt. But they were no longer under his spell.

They had found their inner truth, their inner light, and it shielded them from his manipulations.

In a synchronized motion, Jacob and Evelyn raised their hands, each holding a fragment of the cursed amulet. The jagged pieces glinted ominously, reflecting the remnants of the darkness they had endured.

With a collective surge of strength, they brought the fragments together and, with a resounding crash, shattered the cursed amulet into a thousand pieces.

The moment of impact sent shockwaves through the realm, shaking the very foundation of Puck's power. His once imposing figure trembled, his grip on their minds weakening with each passing second.

He let out a howl of rage and desperation, his illusions crumbling like a fragile façade. As the shards of the amulet scattered across the ground, a blinding light burst forth, illuminating the darkness that had enveloped them.

The light grew in intensity, purging the remnants of Puck's influence and purifying the tainted realm they had traversed. Jacob and Evelyn stood tall amidst the radiant glow, their faces etched with determination and victory.

They had overcome the psychological labyrinth, breaking free from Puck's hold.

Their minds, once clouded by his manipulations, were now clear and resolute.

With Puck's power shattered and his influence extinguished, Jacob and Evelyn turned their backs on him, leaving him to wallow in his own defeat.

They walked away, hand in hand, their souls forever transformed by the trials they had faced.

In the aftermath of their battle, the realm of psychological horror crumbled, replaced by a newfound sense of clarity and freedom.

Jacob and Evelyn emerged stronger, their resilience shining like a beacon of hope for all those who had been ensnared by the manipulations of others.

In the realm of adult psychological horror, their story stands as a chilling reminder of the dangers of manipulation and the importance of cultivating inner strength.

It serves as a call to arms for those who have felt the suffocating grip of psychological control, urging them to tap into their inner resilience and break free from the chains that bind them.

The Seven Ravens

Once upon a time, in a distant village nestled amidst towering mountains, there lived a kind and loving couple named Matthias and Eliza.

They longed for a child to call their own but a curse on the family had stopped them. As time passed Eliza fell with child and it appeared the curse was lifted. and were blessed with seven sons.

The arrival of the seventh son brought great joy to their lives, but fate had a cruel twist in store for them.

But Matthias longed for a daughter, then one day Eliza gave birth to a baby girl.

On the day of the child's christening, a wicked sorceress infiltrated the festivities. Enraged by her exclusion, she cursed the seven son's, transforming them into a raven's and casting them into the vast unknown.

Matthias and Eliza were devastated by the loss of their son's, their lives forever marred by grief and guilt.

Matthias and Eliza were devastated by the loss of their son's, their lives forever marred by grief and guilt.

Eliza's heart was filled with sorrow as she watched the ravens fly away, their cries echoing in the desolate landscape.

The villagers whispered tales of the curse that haunted her family, blaming Eliza for the misfortune that had befallen them. It was in this cauldron of guilt and blame that Eliza's psychological labyrinth was born.

Years passed, and the ravens became a grim symbol of the couple's shattered dreams. Matthias and Eliza's lives were haunted by the memories of their lost child, and the torment of their guilt slowly consumed them.

The village whispered rumours of their cursed existence, their anguish radiating like a dark cloud over their home.

One day, Eliza could bear the weight of her guilt no longer. She made a desperate plea to the heavens, begging for redemption and the chance to bring her lost son back.

To her astonishment, a voice answered her call, promising her a way to reverse the curse and reunite her fractured family.

The voice instructed Eliza to embark on a perilous journey through the treacherous forest, where she would find the means to break the curse that plagued her sons.

Driven by hope and fuelled by the relentless ache in her heart, Eliza set out on her quest, her determination a shield against the dark forces that lurked in the shadows.

As she ventured deeper into the forest, the air grew thick with foreboding, and whispers echoed through the trees. Eliza's steps faltered, her mind haunted by doubts and fears.

But the memory of her lost son's propelled her forward, the unwavering love in her heart providing a flicker of light in the encroaching darkness.

After days of traversing the unforgiving wilderness, Eliza stumbled upon a decrepit cottage, its windows shattered, and its walls veiled in shadows.

An old crone, clad in tattered rags, greeted her with a toothless grin. She introduced herself as Baba Yaga, a notorious sorceress with the power to grant Eliza's deepest desires.

Baba Yaga revealed the arduous task that Eliza must undertake to break the curse. She must gather the feathers of seven ravens, each representing one of her lost sons, and burn them in a sacred fire on the eve of the next full moon.

Only then would the curse be lifted, and her sons restored to their human forms.

Eliza's heart soared with hope, but deep within her, a seed of doubt sprouted. Baba Yaga's demands seemed too great, her motives obscured by a shroud of mystery.

Nevertheless, Eliza, desperate to right her wrongs, agreed to the sorceress's terms, venturing forth into the forest to find the elusive ravens.

The forest became a labyrinth of shadows, its trees twisting and contorting like gnarled fingers reaching out to ensnare her.

Eliza's mind played tricks on her, whispering tales of deceit and betrayal. She felt the weight of her guilt bear down upon her, threatening to crush her spirit.

Amidst the relentless pursuit of the ravens, Eliza encountered ominous figures creatures of the forest who seemed to embody her darkest fears and regrets.

They whispered taunts in her ear, reminding her of her failures and the irreparable damage she had wrought upon her family.

In the heart of the labyrinth, Eliza found her seven sons, still trapped in their raven forms. They looked upon her with eyes filled with forgiveness and love, their presence a reminder that she was not alone in her struggle.

Together, they confronted the sorceress, whose wickedness had ensnared them all.

With each raven she captured, Eliza's mind slipped further into a maelstrom of psychological turmoil. The echoes of her guilt grew louder, drowning out the faint flicker of hope that had driven her this far.

Doubt clouded her every step, as she questioned whether her quest was an act of redemption or a fu-tile attempt to assuage her own guilt.

With her newfound courage, Eliza broke the sorceress's hold over her sons, shattering the curse that had plagued their lives.

As the ravens transformed back into human form, a sense of liberation washed over them. The guilt that had plagued Eliza and her brothers began to dissipate, replaced by a new-found sense of strength and self-acceptance.

As the eve of the full moon approached, Eliza returned to the cottage of Baba Yaga, her heart heavy with uncertainty. She presented the feathers of the ravens she had captured, their obsidian hue casting an eerie glow in the dim light. Baba Yaga cackled with delight, revealing her true intentions.

"You believed you could simply undo the pain you caused, Eliza?" Baba Yaga sneered. "But redemption does not come so easily. Your sons were not the only ones affected by your choices. You, too, must bear the weight of your sins."

In a whirlwind of darkness, Baba Yaga revealed the twisted truth of Eliza's quest.

The ravens were not mere vessels for her sons' souls, but fragments of her own shattered psyche.

By capturing them, Eliza had unwittingly trapped herself in a psychological prison, doomed to relive her guilt and suffering for eternity.

As the truth settled upon her like a suffocating shroud, Eliza's mind fractured, her sanity crumbling un-der the weight of her guilt.

The cottage transformed into a nightmarish realm, its walls closing in on her, trapping her in a psychological labyrinth from which there was no escape.

The once hopeful journey had become a torturous descent into madness, as Eliza confronted her darkest fears and regrets. She was tormented by the echoes of her lost sons' cries, their accusatory gazes searing into her soul.

The line between reality and illusion blurred, and Eliza's mind became a battle-ground of her own making.

In the depths of her despair, Eliza realized that true redemption could not be found in external quests or the whims of sorceresses.

It had to be forged within herself, through acceptance and forgiveness. With her shattered mind as her battlefield, she mustered the strength to confront her guilt head-on.

In a final act of defiance, Eliza faced her fractured psyche, acknowledging her mistakes and embracing her imperfections.

She released the ravens from their cages, freeing herself from the psychological pris-on she had unwittingly created.

With each feather that drifted away, Eliza felt the weight of her guilt lifting, replaced by a glimmer of self-forgiveness.

As dawn broke, Eliza emerged from the nightmarish realm, her mind battered but resilient. She re-turned to her village, forever changed by her harrowing journey.

No longer burdened by the weight of her guilt, she sought to live a life of redemption and compassion, vowing to cherish the bonds she still had and make amends for her past mistakes.

And so, the tale of the seven ravens lingers in the minds of those who hear it, a haunting reminder of the psychological battles we wage within ourselves.

It serves as a cautionary tale, urging us to confront our guilt, face our fears, and seek healing from within. Only then can we break free from the psychological labyrinths that threaten to consume us and find solace in the light of self-acceptance and redemption.

PROLOGUE TO ALICE

In this psychological horror story based on the prologue to Alice's adventures, we delve into the depths of Alice's psyche, where trauma and psychological turmoil have taken root.

The whimsical world she once created has transformed into a dark reflection of her own inner demons, a place where childhood innocence has been corrupted by fear and confusion.

Once upon a time, in a world that teetered on the edge of sanity, there lived a young girl named Alice.

From an early age, Alice found solace in her vivid imagination, a sanctuary she retreated to in order to escape the harsh realities of her existence.

She wove fantastical tales and created whimsical characters within the realms of her mind, finding comfort in the illusion of control that her imagination provided.

Alice's trauma stems from a deep-seated fear of abandonment, triggered by the sudden loss of her parents.

Their absence left a void in her heart, an emptiness that gnawed at her soul and festered with-in her mind.

The prologue to Alice's story becomes a haunting exploration of her psychological journey, as she navigates the twisted corridors of her own subconscious.

Within the distorted reality of her mind, Alice encounters strange and unsettling characters.

The Cheshire Cat, once a whimsical companion, now becomes a sinister presence, taunting her with riddles that mirror her own inner turmoil.

The Mad Hatter, once a symbol of eccentricity, transforms into a demented figure, whispering cryptic messages that trigger her deepest fears.

As Alice ventures further into the recesses of her mind, she encounters the Queen of Hearts, a tyrant ruling over a realm of chaos and cruelty.

The Queen embodies Alice's own suppressed anger and resentment, a manifestation of the darkness that lurks within her. Alice must confront the Queen and the emotions she represents, battling against the oppressive forces that threaten to consume her.

In her journey, Alice grapples with distorted memories, fragmented glimpses of her past that intertwine with her present reality.

She experiences moments of time dilation, where minutes stretch into hours and hours compress into mere seconds.

The boundaries of space warp and twist, as rooms expand and shrink, reflecting Alice's disoriented perception of the world around her.

Throughout her odyssey, Alice battles with her own identity, questioning who she truly is and struggling to maintain a sense of self.

She is confronted by her own reflection, an alter ego that challenges her beliefs and taunts her with self-doubt. The mirror becomes a portal into the darkest corners of her mind, reflecting the fragmented pieces of her shattered psyche.

The horror of Alice's journey lies not only in the surreal and macabre imagery she encounters but also in the emotional depth of her trauma.

The story delves into the depths of her fear, anxiety, and despair, exploring the psychological scars that haunt her every thought.

It reveals the lasting impact of child-hood trauma and the resilience required to confront and overcome it.

As Alice confronts her fears and battles the twisted manifestations of her trauma, she begins to reclaim her identity and find a glimmer of hope amidst the darkness.

She learns that true strength lies in accepting one's past, embracing vulnerability, and finding the courage to confront the demons that lurk within.

In the annals of adult psychological horror, Alice's story stands as a chilling reminder of the power of the human mind and the profound impact of trauma.

It serves as a cautionary tale, urging us to con-front our own psychological wounds, to navigate the treacherous corridors of our subconscious, and to emerge stronger on the other side.

And so, the prologue to Alice's adventures becomes a harrowing tale of psychological horror, where reality bends, time distorts, and identity fractures. It invites us to venture into the depths of our own minds, to confront our fears and unravel the mysteries that lie within.

THE KING OF THE GOLDEN RIVER

In the cursed village nestled within the Austrian Alps, the psychological torment inflicted upon the villagers by the curse of The King of the Golden River was unrelenting.

The curse had seeped into the very fabric of their lives, creating an atmosphere of fear, despair, and trauma that pervaded every interaction and decision.

The villagers, once a tight-knit community, now lived in constant paranoia and suspicion. They became consumed by their own fears, unable to trust even their closest neighbours.

The curse twisted their perceptions, causing innocent encounters to be perceived as threats and acts of kindness as hidden motives. Nightmares plagued their sleep; each dream a vivid reminder of their deepest insecurities and traumas.

The curse exploited their vulnerabilities, dredging up buried memories and painful experiences, leaving them raw and exposed.

The villagers woke up drenched in cold sweat, haunted by the remnants of their subconscious torment.

The curse also preyed upon their sense of self-worth, amplifying their innermost doubts and insecurities.

The villagers were tormented by relentless self-criticism, their minds filled with a cacophony of voices telling them they were unworthy, unlovable, and irreparably damaged.

The curse fed off their self-doubt, fuelling a cycle of despair that seemed impossible to break.

As the curse intensified, hallucinations plagued the villagers. They saw apparitions of their deepest fears and regrets manifesting before their eyes.

The villagers were forced to confront the ghosts of their past, their darkest secrets exposed for all to see. The torment became suffocating, as they struggled to differentiate between reality and the illusions created by their own shattered psyches.

The curse also targeted their relationships, tearing apart families and friendships. The villagers became isolated, trapped in their own mental prisons.

They longed for connection, yet the curse made it impossible to trust or form genuine bonds.

The emotional toll was devastating, leaving them feeling utterly alone in their suffering.

Children were not spared from the curse's psychological torment. Their innocent minds were twisted by the curse, turning them into vessels of fear and anxiety.

They carried the weight of the village's collective trauma, unable to comprehend the darkness that surrounded them.

Their once-playful laughter was replaced by nervous whispers and haunted glances.

Amidst the chaos, three siblings, Hans, Gretchen, and Karl, find themselves at the centre of the village's turmoil. Orphaned at a young age, they had grown up in the shadow of the curse, their lives filled with hardship and loss.

But they possessed a glimmer of hope a belief that they could break the curse and bring prosperity back to their people.

Driven by their shared determination, the siblings embark on a perilous journey to uncover the secrets of the Golden River.

They face harrowing trials and encounter grotesque creatures that embody their innermost fears and insecurities. Each sibling must confront their own personal demons and make sacrifices along the way.

As Hans, the eldest, battles with his insatiable thirst for power and wealth, he is confronted by a golden spectre a twisted version of himself consumed by greed.

The spectre taunts him, whispering promises of untold riches and unbridled power.

Hans must confront his own desires and reconcile with the darkness that lies within.

Gretchen, the middle sibling, grapples with her deep-seated fear of failure and rejection. She encounters a spectral figure, a reflection of her own self-doubt and insecurity.

The figure taunts her with haunting whispers, reminding her of past mistakes and filling her with paralyzing self-doubt.

Gretchen must find the strength to overcome her fears and embrace her inner resilience.

Karl, the youngest of the siblings, battles with his overwhelming sense of guilt and responsibility.

He is plagued by visions of his deceased parents, their accusing stares piercing his soul. Karl must confront his past actions and make amends, seeking forgiveness within himself and from those he has wronged.

As the siblings venture deeper into the heart of the cursed valley, they encounter the mysterious King of the Golden River, a spectral figure who holds the key to their salvation.

The King presents them with a choice a selfless act of sacrifice that will break the curse and restore balance to the land.

In a climactic showdown, the siblings are forced to confront their own deepest fears and desires.

They must navigate a psychological labyrinth, where reality shifts and their perceptions are distorted.

The villagers, trapped in their own personal nightmares, must confront the consequences of their actions, and find redemption.

In a final act of selflessness and unity, the siblings make the ultimate sacrifice.

They offer them-selves as vessels to absorb the curse, allowing the golden waters to wash away their own pain and suffering. Through their sacrifice, the curse is lifted, and the valley is transformed into a place of healing and growth.

As the curse lifted, the village slowly began to heal.

The twisted landscapes reverted to their natural beauty, and the villagers found solace in their new-found unity and compassion.

The legend of The King of the Golden River became a cautionary tale, a reminder of the destructive nature of greed and the redemptive power of empathy.

And so, the tale of The King of the Golden River serves as a chilling reminder of the darkness that can consume even the most seemingly idyllic landscapes.

It explores the depths of human desire and the psychological toll that unchecked ambition can exact. It is a cautionary tale that urges us to examine our own motivations and find balance between material wealth and the richness of the human spirit.

As we navigate the treacherous waters of our own desires, let us remember the lessons learned from The King of the Golden River a tale of horror and redemption that reminds us of the power of empathy and the enduring strength of the human spirit.

The King of Persia and the Princess of the Sea

Once upon a time, in the enchanting land of Persia, there lived a young king named Shahryar.

He was a man consumed by darkness, his heart scarred by betrayal and deceit. His reign was marked by tyranny and cruelty, as he sought to protect himself from the pain he had endured.

In his pursuit of power and control, Shahryar had vowed to never trust a woman again.

To ensure his safety, he married a new bride each night, only to have her executed at dawn. The women of the kingdom lived in constant fear, their lives expendable in the king's twisted game.

One fateful night, a young princess named Zahra found herself chosen as Shahryar's bride.

She was unlike any woman the king had encountered before intelligent, independent, and unafraid to challenge his oppressive rule.

Zahra possessed a mystical connection to the sea, for she was the Princess of the Sea herself.

As Zahra entered the king's chambers, a veil of darkness descended upon her.

The room transformed into a twisted labyrinth of horrors, mirroring the depths of Shahryar's troubled mind.

The walls breathed with whispers; the air heavy with the weight of past atrocities.

Unbeknownst to Shahryar, Zahra had the power to navigate the darkness that consumed him. She possessed the ability to delve into the depths of his psyche, confronting the traumas and demons that haunted him.

Zahra saw beyond the façade of the ruthless king, recognizing the wounded soul that lay beneath.

In the labyrinth of Shahryar's mind, Zahra encountered fragmented memories and suppressed emotions. She witnessed the betrayal that had scarred him, the loss that had hardened his heart.

Each step in the labyrinth revealed a layer of his pain, bringing them closer to the truth. As Zahra ventured further into the labyrinth of Shahryar's mind, she encountered the depths of his psychological torment.

The traumas he had endured had left indelible scars, shaped his perception of the world, and fuelled his cruelty.

Zahra witnessed Shahryar's childhood, marred by betrayal and abandonment. His own father had cast him aside, leaving him vulnerable to the machinations of those who sought to exploit his vulnerability.

The wounds of his past festered within him, poisoning his trust and distorting his ability to form meaningful connections. In the labyrinth, Zahra discovered memories of Shahryar's first love, a woman who had betrayed him in the most unimaginable way.

The pain of her betrayal had seared his soul, leaving him incapable of opening his heart to another.

The trauma of lost love and broken trust had driven him to build walls around himself, ensuring he would never again be vulnerable to such devastating pain.

As she delved deeper, she encountered Shahryar's internal struggle with guilt and shame. The weight of his actions as a tyrannical ruler weighed heavily on his conscience, causing him to question his own humanity.

The cries of the innocent women he had condemned to death echoed in his mind, tormenting him day and night.

The psychological torment took the form of relentless nightmares that plagued Shahryar's sleep. He was haunted by visions of the faces of those he had wronged, their eyes filled with fear and accusation.

Each night, he was confronted with the consequences of his actions, unable to escape the torment even in his dreams.

Zahra saw the fractured psyche of a man torn between his desire for power and his yearning for redemption. The conflicting emotions waged a constant battle within him, tearing at his sanity.

Shahryar's mind became a battleground, where guilt, anger, and self-loathing fought for control, leaving him trapped in a cycle of torment.

With each revelation, Zahra's compassion grew. She recognized that Shahryar's cruelty was not born out of malice, but out of his own deeply rooted pain.

She saw the wounded child within the tyrant, desperately seeking validation and love, yet unable to break free from the cycle of trauma that had shaped him.

She became Shahryar's guiding light, offering him empathy, and understanding.

She helped him confront his darkest memories and face the demons that haunted him.

Through her unwavering support, she encouraged him to acknowledge his own pain and take steps towards healing.

As the psychological torment intensified; Shahryar's defences began to crumble. The walls he had erected around his heart cracked, allowing the light of Zahra's compassion to seep in.

The realization that he had perpetuated the very pain he had endured awakened a profound sense of remorse and a burning desire for redemption.

Together, Zahra and Shahryar embarked on a journey of self-discovery and healing. They confronted their shared traumas, providing solace and support to one another.

Through their connection, Shahryar found the strength to face his past, seek forgiveness, and strive to become a better ruler, husband, and human being.

The tale of The King of Persia and the Princess of the Sea explores the depths of psychological torment, highlighting the transformative power of empathy, understanding, and self-reflection.

It emphasizes the importance of confronting one's own trauma to break free from the cycle of pain and create a path towards healing.

THE SIX SWANS

In the depths of an ancient forest, a young queen named Elowen found herself ensnared in a web of dark enchantment.

Her husband, the king, had gone off to wage a distant war, leaving her alone to care for their six young sons. Little did she know that a malevolent sorceress had set her sights on the royal family, intent on unleashing her twisted magic upon their lives.

One fateful day, as Elowen walked through the forest, she stumbled upon the sorceress's hidden lair.

Enraged by the queen's intrusion, the sorceress cast a wicked spell, turning the six princes into swans, and binding them to the skies until a specific condition was met.

Only Elowen held the key to their salvation, for she had to weave six magical shirts made from stinging nettles and remain completely silent throughout the process.

Failure to complete the task would doom her sons to a life of eternal avian captivity.

The sorceress's curse weighed heavily on Elowen's heart. She felt the weight of her sons' fate pressing down upon her, and the trauma of their transformation seeped into her very being.

Consumed by guilt and grief, Elowen embarked on a treacherous journey to find the elusive stinging nettles, her mind clouded by the horrors she had witnessed.

As Elowen ventured deeper into the forest, the trees seemed to whisper with sinister intent. Shadows danced and twisted, mocking her as she stumbled through the undergrowth.

Her mind played tricks on her, conjuring haunting visions of her swan-princes suffering, their feathers-stained crimson with their mother's tears.

The queen's journey was not only a physical trial but a psychological descent into darkness.

The relentless torment of guilt gnawed at her conscience, unravelling her sanity with each passing day.

Sleep became a distant memory, for her dreams were plagued by nightmarish visions of her sons trapped in their avian forms, their eyes pleading for release from their feathery prison.

Elowen's mental anguish was exacerbated by the incessant whispers of the sorceress, who taunted her from the shadows.

The sorceress's voice echoed in her mind, a constant reminder of the terrible price her family had paid for her intrusion.

The queen's psyche became a battleground for conflicting emotions and love for her sons, anger at her own helplessness, and the all-consuming desire to break the curse.

The queen's harrowing journey led her to a secluded glade where the stinging nettles grew.

But gathering the nettles proved treacherous, as their sharp thorns pierced her hands, mingling her blood with their poisonous sting.

Each prick of pain intensified the darkness within Elowen, feeding her growing obsession with completing the task at any cost.

Days turned into weeks, and the queen's once regal appearance withered as she worked tirelessly to weave the shirts. The nettles stung her raw and bloodied hands, but she persisted, driven by a single-minded determination that bordered on madness.

She could not bear the thought of her sons languishing in their avian forms any longer.

As Elowen neared the completion of the final shirt, the psychological toll of her ordeal reached its peak.

The trauma and isolation had fractured her mind, and she teetered on the edge of sanity.

Whispers of doubt echoed in her ears, sowing seeds of self-destruction. Her once gentle nature twisted into some-thing darker and more primal, as the lines between her identity and the sorceress's malevolence blurred.

Finally, the last shirt was woven, a testament to Elowen's unyielding determination. But in her obsessive pursuit, she had become deaf to her own voice.

Silence had become her only companion, eroding her ability to communicate, both with herself and the outside world. The psychological barriers she had erected threatened to trap her in a self-imposed silence, forever cut off from the world she longed to save.

In a climactic moment of truth, Elowen faced the ultimate test.

She stood before her transformed sons; the final shirt clutched in her trembling hands.

With a heart heavy with love and fear, she wrapped each swan-prince in their respective garment. The air crackled with anticipation as she held her breath, willing the curse to break.

As the last shirt was placed upon the youngest prince, a dazzling light engulfed the clearing.

Feathers fell away, and in their place stood six handsome princes, their eyes filled with both gratitude and the indelible mark of their shared trauma.

The curse was broken, but the psychological scars remained, etched into the hearts and minds of mother and sons.

In the aftermath of their release, Elowen's mind teetered on the edge of madness.

The weight of the curse had taken its toll, and she struggled to find solace in the world she had fought so hard to save.

Nightmares plagued her sleep, and she was haunted by the spectre of her own descent into darkness.

The tale of The Six Swans serves as a chilling reminder of the psychological and emotional toll that trauma can inflict upon the human mind.

It explores the depths of a mother's love and the lengths to which she will go to protect her children.

The queen's journey showcases the indomitable strength of the human spirit and the resilience required to navigate the labyrinth of one's own psyche.

Beauty and The Beast

Once upon a time, in a forgotten corner of the world, there lived a young woman named Isabella. She was a beauty, with cascading golden locks and eyes that sparkled like emeralds.

But Isabella's life was far from idyllic. She was plagued by a darkness that overshadowed her every step a darkness that had been etched into her soul by a traumatic event from her past.

Years before Isabella's encounter with the Beast, she lived in a small village nestled in the shadow of the cursed forest.

Her family was loving and close-knit, and life seemed blissful. But one fateful night, tragedy struck.

The village was engulfed in flames, its streets consumed by a raging inferno. Amidst the chaos, Isabella's world had been shattered.

She witnessed her parents perish in the flames; their anguished cries etched into her memory forever.

The traumatic loss left her orphaned and scarred; her spirit broken by the magnitude of the tragedy.

Survivors guilt gnawed at her soul, leaving her with a profound sense of emptiness and a haunting question:

Why had she been spared when so many others had perished?

Isabella became plagued by recurring nightmares that replayed the horrifying events of the fire.

The images of the engulfed village, the desperate cries for help, and the feeling of helplessness haunted her every waking moment.

Flashbacks would overwhelm her unexpectedly, triggering intense feelings of fear, anxiety, and grief. The trauma had rewired her brain, leaving her in a constant state of hyper-arousal, always on edge and anticipating danger.

The trauma of that night embedded itself deep within Isabella's psyche, casting a long and dark shadow over her life.

She struggled with survivor's guilt, plagued by nightmares that transported her back to the night of the fire.

The smell of smoke haunted her senses, and the crackling of flames echoed in her ears, a constant reminder of the tragedy that had befallen her family and community.

As Isabella grew older, the weight of her trauma became unbearable. She withdrew from the world, building walls around her heart to protect herself from the pain.

She lost her sense of identity, her purpose in life, as the guilt and grief consumed her. Each day was a battle, and the scars from the fire served as a constant reminder of the darkness that had engulfed her world.

As time passed Isabella's Mother remarried and her Stepfather was once a wealthy merchant who had now fallen upon hard times.

Desperate to restore his fortune, he ventured into a mysterious and fore-boding forest, hoping to find a rare treasure that could change their lives. Unbeknownst to him, the forest was cursed a haunting place where nightmares were born and the boundary between reality and the supernatural blurred.

Deep within the heart of the forest, Isabella's father stumbled upon a hidden castle.

Its grandeur was undeniable, but its walls were marred by decay and neglect. Curiosity gripped him, and he couldn't resist exploring the eerie chambers that lay within.

In a forgotten room, he came face to face with a fearsome beast an embodiment of darkness, with piercing yellow eyes and fangs that dripped with venom.

Terrified, Isabella's stepfather attempted to flee, but he was ensnared by the Beast's wrath.

In exchange for his freedom, he made a terrible bargain he promised to send Isabella to live with the Beast in his cursed castle.

Heartbroken and desperate to protect her father, Isabella agreed to the arrangement, her life forever entwined with the darkness that lurked within the castle's walls.

As Isabella arrived at the castle, she was greeted by a world of perpetual gloom and eerie silence. The Beast, shrouded in mystery, seemed to embody the very essence of her deepest fears and insecurities.

His voice, a growl that reverberated through the corridors, sent shivers down her spine.

Yet beneath the fearsome exterior, Isabella sensed a glimmer of humanity an inner struggle that mirrored her own.

Isabella gradually opened her heart to the Beast; she discovered that vulnerability and connection were the keys to her liberation.

She learned to trust again, to let go of the guilt that had bound her, and to embrace the beauty that lay within her scars. Through the Beast's unwavering support and love, she found the strength to rebuild her shattered identity and to reclaim her life.

Days turned into weeks, and weeks into months, as Isabella became trapped in the labyrinthine depths of the castle.

The Beast, driven by an insatiable longing for connection, sought to break through the walls that she had erected around her heart.

He presented her with gifts, lavished her with riches, and attempted to win her over with grand gestures.

But Isabella remained guarded, haunted by the trauma that had consumed her soul.

Within the castle's walls, Isabella found herself caught in a psychological labyrinth, where she was forced to confront the darkest corners of her mind.

The Beast, while initially a representation of her fears and trauma, also became a catalyst for her healing. Their complex dynamic mirrored the internal struggle between vulnerability and self-protection that Isabella wrestled with daily.

The Beast's transformation was a mirror to Isabella's own transformation, symbolizing her journey from victim to survivor, from fear to empowerment.

However, this process was not without its challenges.

Isabella's deeply ingrained belief in her own unworthiness and the persistent guilt kept her from fully embracing the Beast's love and accepting her own self-worth.

The psychological trauma she carried continued to influence her perceptions, causing her to doubt her own capacity for happiness and connection.

Through her encounters with other characters within the castle, Isabella was confronted with reflections of her own psychological struggles.

The enchanted household objects, each with their own stories of pain and suffering, served as poignant reminders of the complexities of trauma and its far-reaching effects.

Isabella's interactions with these characters allowed her to develop a deeper understanding of her own trauma and the shared experiences of others who had also endured great hardship.

As Isabella's journey continued, she gradually peeled back the layers of her trauma, unravelling the tangled threads that had kept her captive for so long.

It was a painful process of self-discovery, filled with moments of anguish and resistance.

But with each step, she gained a greater understanding of the ways in which her trauma had shaped her perceptions, beliefs, and relationships.

Ultimately, Isabella's trans-formation was not about erasing her traumatic past but rather about reclaiming her power and finding meaning in her pain.

Through therapy and the support of the Beast and the enchanted household, she learned to integrate her trauma into her identity without allowing it to define her.

She discovered that her strength and resilience was born from her experiences, and that her capacity for love and connection could transcend the darkness that had consumed her.

sabella's story serves as a poignant exploration of the profound impact of psychological trauma and the intricate journey of healing and self-discovery.

Through her struggles and triumphs, readers are invited to reflect on their own experiences of trauma and find solace in the possibility of growth, resilience, and the reclamation of one's true self.

May Isabella's story be a guiding light for those who have endured psychological trauma, reminding them that their pain does not define them and that healing, and transformation is possible, even in the darkest of times.

The Princess and the Pea

Once upon a time, in a kingdom shrouded in darkness, there lived a king obsessed with finding a true princess to wed his son and secure the royal bloodline.

The king, known for his callous nature, devised a plan to test the authenticity of every potential princess who sought the prince's hand.

One stormy night, a young woman named Cecilia arrived at the castle, claiming to be a princess. She sought refuge from the tempest that raged outside, hoping to find solace within the castle walls.

The king, sceptical of her claims, agreed to put her to the test.

In a chamber atop a towering tower, a bed was prepared for Cecilia. Beneath the sumptuous layers of mattresses and exquisite bedding, a single pea was hidden.

The king believed that only a true princess, possessing extraordinary sensitivity, would be able to detect the discomfort caused by the tiny pea.

As Cecilia lay upon the bed, her senses heightened by the anticipation and the eerie atmosphere of the castle, she began to feel an inexplicable discomfort.

The pea, seemingly insignificant, tortured her body and mind. Night after night, she lay awake, tormented by the relentless discomfort caused by the hidden pea.

Days turned into weeks, and Cecilia's health began to deteriorate. The sleepless nights, coupled with the relentless psychological torment, took a toll on her psyche.

She became consumed by paranoia and anxiety, convinced that the entire kingdom was watching her, waiting for her to fail the test.

As Cecilia's torment continued, the weight of the hidden pea became an ever-present burden on her mind.

The physical discomfort extended into her psyche, triggering a cascade of psychological trauma that entangled her thoughts and emotions.

The once vibrant and confident princess became consumed by self-doubt and fear. Sleep, which should have provided respite, became an arena of nightmares for Cecilia.

She would toss and turn in bed, unable to escape the relentless torment.

The pea, though small in size, grew in her mind, morphing into a symbol of her inadequacy and worthlessness. Dreams turned into twisted scenes of judgment and rejection, where she was constantly tested and found lacking.

The courtiers, aware of Cecilia's inner struggles, exploited her vulnerabilities, further intensifying her trauma.

They revelled in her suffering, using every opportunity to belittle and humiliate her.

Their cruel taunts and mocking laughter echoed in her mind, reinforcing her insecurities, and confirming her deepest fears. Isolation became Cecilia's refuge.

She sought solace in the confines of her chamber, barricading herself from the prying eyes and judgmental gazes of the court.

But within the walls of her solitude, the darkness loomed larger. The silence grew deafening, amplifying the whispers of self-doubt that plagued her mind.

Her reflection in the mirror became an adversary, an embodiment of all her perceived flaws and failures. Every imperfection was magnified, every flaw a glaring reminder of her supposed unworthiness.

She questioned her own identity, wondering if she truly belonged in the royal court or if she was an imposter trapped in a web of lies.

Fear and paranoia gnawed at Cecilia's sanity. She became hyperaware of the scrutinizing eyes that followed her every move.

Even innocent gestures and words became loaded with hidden meanings, feeding her growing sense of persecution. She questioned the motives of those around her, never certain of their true intentions.

But amid the darkness, flickers of resilience emerged within Cecilia's soul.

A fire ignited, fuelling her determination to break free from the shackles of her trauma.

She sought solace in books, losing herself in tales of strength and resilience.

She found companionship in the pages, connecting with characters who had faced their own trials and triumphed over adversity.

Slowly, Cecilia started to seek professional help. A wise counsellor, well-versed in the complexities of trauma, became her guiding light. Through therapy, she untangled the web of distorted beliefs and shattered self-esteem.

Together, they delved into the roots of her trauma, excavating buried pain, and addressing the wounds that had festered for far too long.

As the layers of trauma peeled away, Cecilia's true strength began to emerge. She discovered her voice, no longer silenced by fear and self-doubt. She spoke her truth, defying the expectations and judgments of others.

With every step forward, she reclaimed fragments of her shattered identity, slowly piecing her-self back together. Healing was not linear, however.

Cecilia faced setbacks and relapses along her journey. The ghosts of the trauma occasionally resurfaced, triggering old wounds and unsettling memories. But armed with newfound resilience, she pressed on, refusing to let her past define her future.

In time, Cecilia's resilience and newfound sense of self radiated like a beacon, inspiring others who had endured similar traumas.

She became an advocate for mental health, using her own experience to raise awareness and foster empathy.

Her story became a testament to the strength of the human spirit and the transformative power of healing.

Cecilia's story serves as a haunting reminder of the lasting impact of psychological trauma.

It delves into the complexities of the human mind, shedding light on the ways in which trauma distorts perception, erodes self-worth, and stifles growth.

HANSEL AND GRETEL

Once upon a time, in a dark and foreboding forest, there lived two siblings named Hansel and Gretel.

They were but children, innocent and full of curiosity, until a series of unfortunate events led them to a place of nightmares.

Hansel, the older of the two, was burdened with the responsibility of protecting his younger sister, Gretel.

They were born into a family plagued by poverty and hardship, their parents struggling to provide even the barest necessities of life.

With each passing day, the weight of their circumstances bore down on the siblings, filling their hearts with a sense of hopelessness.

One fateful day, as their stomachs growled with hunger, their parents made a decision that would change the course of their lives.

Unable to bear the burden of caring for them any longer, they devised a plan to abandon Hansel and Gretel in the heart of the forest, believing it was their only chance for survival.

Lost and alone, the siblings ventured deeper into the labyrinthine woods, their tiny hands clasped tightly together.

They followed a trail of breadcrumbs, a meagre attempt to mark their path, but the birds of the forest had other plans. With each step, the breadcrumbs disappeared, leaving them truly lost and at the mercy of the wilderness.

As the sun sank below the horizon, the forest transformed into a sinister realm, casting eerie shadows, and whispering secrets of the unknown.

Fear gripped their hearts as they stumbled upon a clearing, only to find themselves standing before a peculiar cottage made entirely of gingerbread and candy.

The aroma of sugary delights filled the air as Hansel and Gretel approached the enchanting cottage made entirely of sweets.

Their eyes widened with both hunger and wonder, drawn to the tantalizing display of candy canes, gingerbread walls, and chocolate roof tiles.

It seemed like a dream come true, a respite from their harsh reality.

Driven by their insatiable hunger, Hansel and Gretel hesitantly reached out and plucked a piece of candy from the walls.

As soon as the sweet confection touched their lips, a wave of euphoria washed over them.

The Flavours exploded in their mouths, momentarily erasing the hardships they had endured.

But little did they know that the house of sweets was not what it seemed.

It was a trap, meticulously designed by the witch who resided within. Her plan was to lure unsuspecting children into her clutches, using their desperation for nourishment as a tool for her own sinister desires.

As Hansel and Gretel indulged in the sugary delights, a sense of unease crept over them. The once inviting cottage now felt suffocating, its walls closing in on them.

The vibrant colours seemed to dull, taking on a sickly hue.

The very air grew heavy with a foreboding presence.

The witch, disguised as a kindly old woman, revealed herself from behind the candy-coated doorway.

Her eyes gleamed with wicked delight, knowing that she had captured her prey. With a twisted smile, she beckoned Hansel and Gretel inside, promising them more treats and a life of abundance.

As Hansel and Gretel cautiously entered the cottage, they were greeted by the witch, her smile as sweet as honey, yet her intentions as dark as night. She promised them warmth, shelter, and an endless sup-ply of food.

It seemed like a dream come true, a refuge from the harsh realities they had faced.

Unaware of the danger that lurked, the siblings stepped into the witch's domain. The interior of the cottage was a macabre spectacle, a juxtaposition of sweetness and horror.

The walls, once adorned with candy, now dripped with a sticky, crimson substance that resembled blood.

But the witch's true nature soon revealed itself. She cackled with glee, revealing her sinister plan to fatten up the children and devour them like a predator feasting on its prey.

Hansel and Gretel were trapped in her clutches, victims of their own desperate hunger.

Fear consumed them, gnawing at their minds and weakening their resolve.

They were trapped in a house of nightmares, where every corner held a sinister secret. The once-enticing candy became a symbol of their impending demise, a reminder of their vulnerability and the darkness that lay within seemingly innocent things.

The air grew thick with an otherworldly presence, and the sweet scent turned sickly, mingling with the stench of decay.

The witch's true form was revealed; a haggard figure with gnarled limbs and a twisted smile that sent shivers down their spines.

Her true intentions were far from benevolent.

With a cackling laugh, the witch revealed her insidious plan. Hansel would be fattened up and devoured, while Gretel would be enslaved, forced to serve the witch's every whim.

The siblings' momentary reprieve turned into a nightmare of unimaginable proportions.

As the realization of their impending doom sank in, panic gripped Hansel and Gretel. They scrambled to find an escape, their hearts pounding in their chests.

But the witch's magic was powerful, and her grip on them tightened. They were trapped, prisoners in a house that promised sweetness but concealed unspeakable horrors.

Days turned into weeks, and the children languished in the witch's clutches, subjected to her torment and cruelty.

They were forced to toil in the kitchen, preparing lavish meals that would ultimately be their own undoing.
The witch revelled in their suffering, relishing every moment of their anguish.

But deep within the hearts of Hansel and Gretel, a flicker of determination remained.

They refused to succumb to the witch's wickedness, clinging to the hope of escape.

They plotted and planned; their minds sharpened by the horrors they had witnessed.

In a final act of desperation, Hansel devised a plan to outwit the witch. He pretended to be weak and feeble, convincing her that he needed more time to fatten up.

Day by day, he surreptitiously collected small stones, creating a breadcrumb trail that would lead them back home.

As the witch prepared her cauldron, ready to cook Hansel to satisfy her insatiable appetite, Gretel mustered the last vestiges of her strength. She knew they had to act swiftly, or they would be lost for-ever.

With determination burning in her eyes, she whispered a plan to her brother, hoping against hope that it would lead them to freedom.

Together, they devised a daring escape, using their wits and agility to outsmart the witch.

In a final act of defiance, they pushed her into her own cauldron, watching as her malevolence was consumed by the very darkness she had summoned.

In a moment of confusion Hansel managed to outwit the witch and free himself and Gretel, running as fast as they could back into the forest.

The air was thick with tension as Hansel and Gretel found themselves locked in a desperate battle for survival.

In the depths of the enchanted forest, they encountered a new terror a pack of ferocious creatures that lurked in the shadows, hungry for their flesh.

With every step, the siblings could feel the weight of their fear pressing upon them.

The forest seemed to come alive, the trees whispering ominous warnings and the leaves rustling with malicious intent.

They knew they had to stay alert, relying on their instincts and each other to navigate this treacherous terrain.

The creatures, with their razor-sharp claws and fangs, were relentless in their pursuit. Hansel and Gretel darted through the undergrowth, their hearts pounding, their breaths ragged.

Fear threatened to consume them, but they refused to succumb to its grip. They had fought too hard to escape the clutches of the sorceress to let these creatures undo their progress.

As the moon rose high in the night sky, casting an ethereal glow upon the forest, the siblings found themselves cornered.

Trapped between the gnarled roots of an ancient tree, they faced their attackers head-on. It was a fight for their lives a fight that would test their strength, resilience, and determination to survive.

Hansel swung his makeshift weapon, a sturdy branch, with all his might, striking the creatures with calculated precision.

Gretel, armed with her wits and agility, ducked, and weaved, evading their attacks while launching counterstrike's of her own.

Together, they formed a formidable duo, their bond and shared trauma fuelling their resolve.

Blood stained the forest floor as the battle waged on.

The creatures, driven by a hunger that could not be sated, fought ferociously.

But Hansel and Gretel fought back with a fire that burned within their souls.

Their survival instincts kicked into overdrive, their minds focused on one goal—to emerge victorious and live to see another day.

The fight seemed to stretch on for an eternity, their bodies growing weary, their muscles screaming for respite. But they couldn't afford to give in to exhaustion.

They had come too far to let it all slip away. With a surge of determination, they channelled their pain and trauma, transforming it into a powerful force that propelled them forward.

Finally, the creatures began to falter. Their once-ferocious attacks grew feeble, their movements sluggish.

Hansel and Gretel seized the opportunity, striking with precision and efficiency.

One by one, the creatures fell, their lifeless bodies blending into the eerie landscape.

Breathing heavily, covered in dirt and blood, Hansel and Gretel stood victorious. The forest fell silent, the tension dissipating like smoke in the wind.

They took a moment to catch their breaths, their eyes locking in a silent acknowledgment of their triumph.

As the days turned into weeks and the weeks into months, Hansel and Gretel found themselves living in a constant state of fear. The trauma they had endured at the hands of the wicked witch had left an in-delible mark on their souls, and the power of fear had woven its web around their every thought and action.

No longer did they venture into the forest freely, their once carefree spirits dampened by the lingering shadow of their past.

The rustling leaves and gentle breeze that had once brought them joy now stirred a sense of unease deep within them. The world had become a treacherous place, filled with unseen dangers lurking in the shadows.

Their parents, sensing their children's distress, tried their best to create a sense of safety and security within the confines of their home.

But even the familiar walls of their house offered little solace. The creaking floors and howling wind outside only served to heighten their fears, reminding them of the darkness that had once enveloped their lives.

The psychological trauma depicted in the story can resonate with readers who have experienced similar traumas in their own lives. They may find solace in seeing their own struggles reflected in the characters' journey, validating their emotions, and offering a sense of understanding.

The story can open up a dialogue around trauma, resilience, and healing, encouraging readers to confront their own experiences and seek support when needed.

Through the lens of Hansel and Gretel's trauma, readers can gain insight into the complexities of psychological wounds and the long-lasting effects they can have.

The story invites readers to explore themes of resilience, growth, and the human capacity to overcome adversity. It offers a glimpse into the depths of the human psyche, shedding light on the importance of understanding, compassion, and the power of healing.

Overall, the impact of Hansel and Gretel's psychological trauma in the story can be profound for readers.

It provides a platform for exploring the complexities of trauma, igniting conversations around mental health and resilience.

Through their journey, readers are invited to confront their own fears and find hope in the face of darkness, ultimately leaving them with a deeper understanding of the human experience.

As the final pages of "Whispers of the Enchanting Dark: The Dark Secrets of Fairy Tales" end, the journey through the intricate realms of the human psyche and the hidden secrets of fairy tales leaves an indelible mark on the reader's soul. The tendrils of the enchanting dark continue to weave their way through their thoughts, compelling them to further explore the labyrinthine depths of the human experience.

Throughout the book, we have unravelled the threads of darkness that lie beneath the surface of be-loved fairy tales. We have delved into the intricate webs of fear, trauma, and despair, peering into the haunting landscapes that reside within the collective consciousness. Each tale has offered a glimpse in-to the darker recesses of the human condition, exposing the vulnerabilities, fears, and hidden desires that often remain shrouded in the shadows.

But as we moved deeper into the enchanting dark, we discovered that its essence is not solely rooted in horror and despair. Amidst the chilling narratives and unsettling revelations, there lies a profound opportunity for growth, resilience, and self-discovery. The tales serve as mirrors, reflecting our own journeys of self-exploration and transformation.

In this extended epilogue, I invite you to further reflect upon the impact of the enchanting dark on their own lives. Encouraging you to embrace the shadows as sources of wisdom and insight. For it is in the embrace of darkness that we uncover the hidden truths and deeper meanings that lie beneath the surface.

As you close the final pages of "Whispers of the Enchanting Dark," you might carry a newfound aware-ness of the complexity of the human psyche. The stories you have encountered have stirred emotions, provoked introspection, and illuminated the intricate tapestry of human existence.

But the enchanting dark does not end with the final chapter. Its whispers linger, echoing through the corridors of our minds, guiding us to explore the uncharted territories of our own fears, traumas, and desires.

It urges us to confront our inner demons, to unravel the layers of our own stories, and to find solace in the interconnectedness of the human experience.

The dark secrets of fairy tales serve as lanterns, illuminating the path to self-discovery and personal growth. They remind us that within the depths of our own shadows, there is an opportunity for healing, transformation, and the cultivation of empathy and compassion.

As we bid farewell to the enchanting dark, we do not part ways with fear and trepidation, but with a newfound appreciation for its role in shaping our narratives. We emerge from the shadows, stronger, wiser, and more attuned to the multifaceted nature of our own existence.

And so, dear reader, as you embark on your own journey beyond these pages, may you carry the Whispers of the Enchanting Dark "The Dark Secrets of Fairy Tales" with you. Allow them to guide you through the labyrinth of your own stories, embracing the shadows as catalysts for growth and self-discovery.

For it is in the depths of the enchanting dark that we truly find ourselves, our truest fears and desires laid bare. And it is through our willingness to explore, confront, and embrace these shadows that we emerge, transformed, into the light of a new chapter in our own personal fairy tale.

A Personal Note

My Dear readers,

As I come to the end of this remarkable journey through "Whispers of the Enchanting Dark: The Dark Secrets of Fairy Tales," I am humbled and grateful for your presence.

It has been a profound honour to guide you through the intricate realms of the human psyche and the hidden depths of beloved fairy tales.

I want to take a moment to express my deepest gratitude for your unwavering support and open-mindedness as we explored the darker side of these enchanting tales. It is through your willingness to delve into the depths of human experience that we have embarked on this transformative ad-venture together.

I hope that the pages of this book have stirred something within you, provoking introspection, igniting curiosity, and perhaps even unlocking doors to the secret chambers of your own psyche.

The enchanting dark holds profound lessons and revelations, and I am grateful to have shared them with you. May this journey continue to resonate within your thoughts, sparking conversations and reflections that extend far beyond the pages of this book.

May the whispers of the enchanting dark guide you to new depths of self-awareness and understanding.

Remember, dear readers, that the stories we have explored are not mere fairy tales, but mirrors reflecting the complexities of our own human existence. Embrace the shadows, for within them lie the keys to unlocking profound growth, resilience, and empathy.

Thank you for joining me on this extraordinary odyssey through the enchanted realms of fairy tales and the human psyche. It is my sincerest hope that "Whispers of the Enchanting Dark" has left an indelible mark on your journey, inspiring you to embrace the full spectrum of human experience.

With heartfelt gratitude and warmest wishes,

Angeless Watkins-Gallar

Is this really the end?

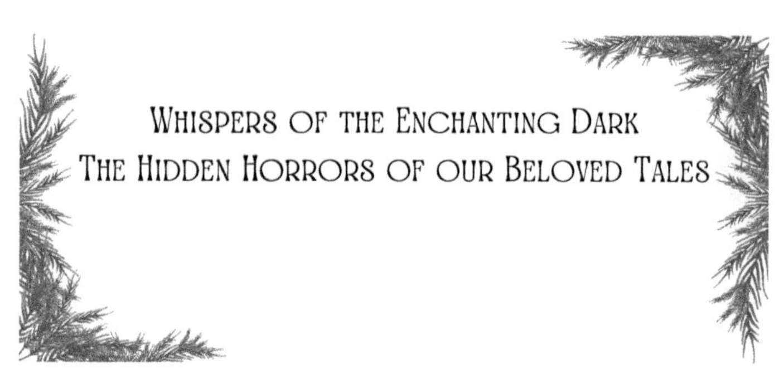

Whispers of the Enchanting Dark
The Hidden Horrors of our Beloved Tales

Whispers of the
Enchanting Dark
The Hidden Horrors of our
Beloved Tales

As the shadows of the night lengthen, and the moon casts an eerie glow over the enchanting forest, I will be inviting you once again to journey with me into the depths of darkness.

In the coming second instalment of Whispers of the Enchanting Dark "The Hidden Horrors of Our Beloved Tales", we delve deeper into the heart of beloved fairy tales, unearthing the hidden horrors that lie beneath their charming facades.

These tales, passed down through generations, have long captivated our imaginations with their magic and wonder. But within the heart of every enchanting story lies a darkness waiting to be unveiled.

As we venture forth together, we will peel back the layers of illusion to reveal the true nature of these haunting tales, exploring the psychological depths and traumas that have lingered within them.

In "The Hidden Horrors of Beloved Tales," we will encounter

"**The Robber Bridegroom**," where deceit and treachery lurk in the shadows, challenging our perceptions of love and trust.
"**The Fisherman and His Wife**," witnessing the destructive allure of insatiable desires and the toll it takes on the human soul.
"**The Enchanted Horse**," we confront the intoxicating allure of boundless power and the psychological struggles it ignites.

Through these chilling stories, we confront the darker aspects of human nature the greed, the obsession, and the insatiable hunger for more.

We delve into the depths of the human psyche, exploring the psychological toll of these tales on both their characters and ourselves.

As we traverse these enchanted landscapes, be prepared to question the very essence of these tales and the impact they have on our own lives.

For within every enchanting story lies a mirror reflecting the deepest corners of our fears and desires.

So, dear reader, brace yourself for the journey ahead.

Let us uncover the hidden horrors of our beloved tales together and may the shadows of these haunting stories leave an indelible mark on your soul. And be prepared to be welcomed to

"Whispers of the Enchanting Dark: The Hidden Horrors of Beloved Tales."

www.ingramcontent.com/pod-product-compliance
Ingram Content Group UK Ltd.
Pitfield, Milton Keynes, MK11 3LW, UK
UKHW021650190726
13853UKWH00001B/174

9 798330 369386